Camilla Way lives in London and, when not writing fiction, works as a journalist. This is her first novel.

THE DEAD OF SUMMER

Following the death of her mother, Anita and her family have moved to a new town, a new home, and a new neighbourhood. The long school holidays are approaching, with summer stretching out before them. Kyle lives across the road from Anita. Cool, surly, laconic, he tells her about the hidden, disused mines: a perfect playground for kids with nothing better to do. But what they don't know is that these mines will be the scene of the most unsettling crime this community has ever known. This summer, everything will change. This summer, the dead days have come home to stay.

CAMILLA WAY

◆

THE DEAD OF SUMMER

Complete and Unabridged

ULVERSCROFT
Leicester

First published in Great Britain in 2007 by
Harper
an imprint of
HarperCollins*Publishers*, London

First Large Print Edition
published 2007
by arrangement with
HarperCollins*Publishers*, London

The moral right of the author has been asserted

This novel is entirely a work of fiction.
The names, characters and incidents portrayed in it
are the work of the author's imagination. Any
resemblance to actual persons, living or dead, events
or localities is entirely coincidental.

'How' by Philip Larkin reproduced by kind
permission of Faber & Faber

British Library CIP Data

Way, Camilla
    The dead of summer.—Large print ed.—
    Ulverscroft large print series: general fiction
    1. Teenagers—England—London—Fiction
    2. Bildungsromans 3. Large type books
    I. Title
    823.9'2 [F]

    ISBN 978–1–84617–787–3

Published by
F. A. Thorpe (Publishing)
Anstey, Leicestershire

Set by Words & Graphics Ltd.
Anstey, Leicestershire
Printed and bound in Great Britain by
T. J. International Ltd., Padstow, Cornwall

This book is printed on acid-free paper

For Dave Holloway,
with love.
And in memory of
Peter Way, my dad.

How

How high they build hospitals!
Lighted cliffs, against dawns
Of days people will die on.
I can see one from here.

How cold winter keeps
And long, ignoring
Our need now for kindness.
Spring has got into the wrong year.

How few people are,
Held apart by acres
Of housing, and children
With their shallow violent eyes.

Philip Larkin

1

Along the back streets, down to the river he took me. Through the wastelands filled with those white flowers, the ones that smell of cats' piss, of summer. Past our hideout, past the warehouses and the factories, almost to the gasworks. Into a scrapyard, not the one we used to play in. And there it was.

By the end of that summer three of us were dead. Tell me, does your pulse quicken when you see those headlines? You know the type: 'Murder Spree of Schoolgirl Loner'; 'Boy, 13, Rapes Classmate'; 'Child, 10, Stabs Pensioner'. Mine too, I've collected them all, over the years. And when you pass those gangs of half-grown ghouls that haunt the streets in the half-light, does your pace quicken just a bit? Do you walk a little faster? It's understandable. Mugging, fighting, raping, killing — kids today, they're animals.

But of all the world's mini-monsters making headlines, wreaking havoc, my friend Kyle was the most famous of all. And I was there. I loved him. Take a seat, Doctor Barton, I'll tell you everything. It's time to tell you everything.

We moved to Myre Street in 1986. I remember I was embarrassed by our crappy furniture. We were so *obviously* the skint Paki family without a pot to piss in, moving it all in by ourselves. So predictable were we with our brown flowery sofa and rubbish telly, sat there in the middle of the street. Plus I was humiliated by my dad's manky old cardi and my sisters' miniskirts and my Auntie Jam in a sari, for Christ's sake.

I knew all the neighbours were watching from their windows. *Knew* they were saying, 'Family moving into 36, dear. Asians by the looks of things. Don't think much of their sofa.' Knew that somewhere, behind one of those nets, someone was laughing at my hair.

I sat on the kerb behind a smashed-up car and willed my brother Push to drop our sofa on his feet while those grand-but-fucked south-London houses crowded and jeered over our row of council homes like playground bullies. I watched my family traipse back and forth with the cardboard boxes that contained our lives and turned away just in time to see Kyle walk out of his gate.

No. 33 Myre Street. 'The House of Horrors'. Big black windows and peeling paint, a roll of carpet rotting amongst the weeds outside. The newspaper men must have been chuffed to bits when they first saw those pictures — the place had 'creepy' written all over it.

And what did I think of Kyle that first day? Not much. I just thought he looked stupid. It was boiling hot and he had an anorak on, zipped right up to his scrawny, birdy neck. And his trousers were too short for his legs. He didn't look at any of us as he walked off down the street but that was the first time I saw Kyle — if that's the sort of thing you're after. He walked off down the street and I didn't see him again until I started school.

The thing you have to remember here is that to everyone else this is a horror story. 'The Events'. 'The Truth Behind The Mines Murders!' But to me it was life. It was just my life. Do you know what I mean? Things happened. Things went wrong. OK, things went very, very, wrong. But at the time it was just us kids — me, Kyle and Denis — just kids knocking about. Because after the questions; after the whats, the whys, the whens, after the outrage and the disbelief, I'm just me, here, without anything I used to have.

* * *

My brother Push and I started school the following Monday. Lewisham High was pretty much just like any other shit-hole south-London comprehensive in the eighties: concrete and kids, wired glass and pissed-off teachers. A forecourt with a broken fountain full of empty crisp bags out front.

When I was introduced to my class and told to take a seat the only place left was next to this fat black kid called Denis. He was the sort of kid who sits alone for good reason. You know when you can just tell without even having to talk to someone, that they're a bit simple? He was the special needs kid, every class has got one. He had National Health glasses thick as car lights and his school uniform was spic and span, his tie too perfectly tied right up to his chin to have done it himself.

I sat down next to him and he turned around, took his specs off, and did this weird thing with his eyes. He sort of peeled the top lid over until the pink under-lid was left so it was just the bloody film. Then he grinned at me like he expected a biscuit or something. I just smiled politely and hoped he'd leave me the fuck alone.

No such luck. I was obviously the only person who had sat next to him in years. I was his new special pal. I was stuck with him.

He knew it, the other kids knew it, and after my first long day with him trailing around after me like my big, fat, black retarded shadow, I knew it too. I didn't really care. I guess I thought that even Denis was better than nothing. I am not someone who makes friends easily either.

Denis wasn't much of a conversationalist. That first day's efforts pretty much went like this.

Me: 'So, Denis! What's the canteen like here?'

Him: 'Do you like the A-Team?'

Me: 'Got any brothers or sisters, Denis?'

Him: 'Have you ever stood on your head until your nose bled?'

But there's something strangely intriguing about having your every question answered by another, totally random one, and by lunchtime I was beginning to enjoy myself.

Me: 'Live near here then, Denis?'

Him: 'Have you got a dog?'

Throughout the day I'd catch glimpses of my brother Push hanging out in the canteen or drifting through corridors between classes. He was clearly throwing himself into Making New Friends. I guess it helped that he was a goodlooking, charming bastard. I just thought he was a bastard. He pretended not to recognise me when Denis and I passed in the hall. I eased my way through that first day, taking in the important landmarks, noting the leaders and the losers while pretty much being shunned by both, and by the time lessons finished for the day it was crystal clear that this school was going to suck just as much as my last one had.

By home time I'd managed to get out of Denis that he lived around the corner from me in Brockley. Assuming this meant I'd be stuck with him for the entire bus journey home, I was actually pretty pissed-off when he seemed mad keen to sidle away by himself as soon as we reached the gates.

'You not catching the 53, then?' I asked, not actually caring, and trying not to sound like I cared, in case he got the wrong idea and thought that I cared. Which I didn't.

Denis shrugged his massive shoulders in his too-tight, shiny blazer, looked at his feet and for once answered my question with a proper answer. 'Gotta wait for Kyle. Gotta wait here till he comes.' Then he looked away, down the street where no one was. A big, dumb smile on his big, dumb face.

I looked down there too, not really knowing how to stick around, then said, 'Oh right. See you later then.' But I stood there for a few minutes longer, swinging my Co-op carrier with its biro sticking out of a hole in the bottom, staring at an ice lolly melting into some dog-shit by my foot. Denis didn't move a muscle or even look at me again. Finally I shrugged and trudged off by myself, not quite able to believe that Denis had any mates and more than a little put out that he didn't want me to hang out with them. Still, he was a retard and his mates were probably retards too, so what did I care? I had better things to do.

As I reached the corner I looked back and saw the skinny white kid from my street walking up to Denis. He was still wearing the anorak. Denis was flapping his arm up and down waving like a lunatic, his big plate of a face beaming like the moon.

*   *   *

That summer of 1986 was hot everywhere in England. In our corner of south-east London the days rolled by in blue and gold, the sun bouncing off the dustbins and burning into windscreens. It lit up our faces, bit at our eyeballs. And when I think about that summer I think of it as like a flaming meteor tearing through empty space. As my bus lurched and heaved through New Cross that first day, my school shirt was damp with sweat and I knew it was going to be a long few months until the holidays began. I wished I had a cigarette.

Seven years ago, that was. When I was a different person. When I was thirteen and still Anita. When I didn't know Kyle.

★ ★ ★

When I was eleven my mother died suddenly of a well-kept secret. One minute she was stirring a pot of rice in our kitchen in Leeds, the next she was crumpled on the floor clutching her left arm. I'm no expert (or maybe I am), but it was a peculiar death, really. I remember at the time I felt a little embarrassed as I laughed, because it was such a strange joke for her to make, on a Monday evening at seven. 'That was rubbish,' I'd said, getting up from my homework for a better look. When it came to fake dying, my mother was clearly in need of advice.

And then I saw her face.

All the things people say about shock aren't true. Time doesn't stand still and you aren't rooted to the spot. What I did do was scream the bloody house down while running like a moron back and forth between her body and the kitchen door. When my father and brother and sisters piled in they found me kneeling, screaming still, trying to shake her awake.

Angina, my Auntie Jam said later. A ticking time-bomb that heart of hers. I wish I'd known. Wish I'd known there were only a certain amount of ticks and tocks my mother's heart had left: I'd have counted every single one.

★   ★   ★

In the months that followed, my family was laid waste. Sadness ate my dad up whole. It wrecked him, battered him, finished him. He walked around or mostly sat in a fairly convincing dad-shaped disguise but behind his staring eyes brain-eating zombies had clearly been at work. We could not reach him. He didn't want us to. Mostly he wanted to drink beer and watch telly in the dark.

And it was easy then for me, Push, Bela and Esha to lose our grip on each other. It was simpler not to hang around the house she had loved us in, her 'milk chocolate buttons', half-Yorkshire, half-Bengali. It was easy not to notice our family unravelling if we were not there to watch.

The months passed and bit by bit Mum's presence faded from the house and the absence of her filled it up. Gradually fewer and fewer envelopes addressed to her landed on the mat; somebody, I don't know who, moved her coat from the hall, her make-up from the bathroom cabinet. With no one to insist on family meals or curfews, no one to keep an eye on what we did with our time, who really noticed when the others stopped bothering to come home at all sometimes or if I forgot to go to school now and then?

* * *

Finally, our Auntie Jam made a stand. Sari swishing with disapproval, Dad was swept into the kitchen for a bollocking. She'd seen Bela coming out of a pub in town, heard rumours that Push was out drinking in the park every night, that Esha was carrying on with the man from the kebabby. As for me, did he even know where I went during the day? Because it certainly wasn't to school. Her scandalised voice hissed from under the kitchen door as I hung over the banister. Silly cow, I thought. With every outraged word, the subtext was clear. If Dad had done the decent thing and married a Bengali woman in the first place, none of this would have happened. Even in death my mother was an embarrassment and now her miserable half-white kids were dragging the family down even further. Enough was enough. Besides, she had plans for our house.

It's fair to say, by the time Dad pulled himself together sufficiently to let Auntie Jam talk him into swapping our shitty council house in Leeds for her mate's even shittier one in London, the Naidus were not winning any prizes for 'Most Together Family of the Year'.

★   ★   ★

After that first day at Lewisham High, I came home to find Push and Dad watching telly in the lounge. They were each sitting on an unpacked cardboard box eating rice crispies, last night's dinner plates and Dad's empty beer cans round their feet.

If your mansion house needs haunting just call Rentaghost,
We've got spooks and ghouls and freaks and fools at Rentaghost . . .

When he saw me in the doorway Push said, 'All right Nitty-no-tits? Saw you with your new fella today.' He grinned into his rice crispies. 'Got yourself a catch there, haven't you?'

Hear the phantom of the opera sing a haunting melody,

11

Remember what you see is not a mystery, but Rentaghost!

'Yeah,' I said. 'Funny,' I said, and went upstairs. In our room Esha and Bela were getting ready to go out. Picking my way through a fug of hairspray, over puddles of jeans and knickers, shoes and bras, I sat down on my bed to watch. 'Mind out, Nit.' Esha used my head to steady herself as she climbed up next to me. Her arms held out for balance, she looked at herself in the half mirror hanging opposite, giggling as Bela got up too, pretend-surfing as they wobbled about on my duvet in their white stilettos.

My older sisters are beautiful and so is Push. ('Poor Anita,' my Auntie Jam said once, giving me the evil eye.) Skin like Bourbon biscuits, they had black hair to their bums (I'd hacked mine off with the kitchen scissors when I was nine) and Mum's wide, green eyes. *Desperately Seeking Susan* was their favourite film and they wore white lace fingerless gloves and black Ray-Bans and a shedload of red lipstick. Deadly, in other words: the blokes of Lewisham didn't stand a chance.

I fiddled about with our pink radio-alarm clock, twiddling the knob between stations, listening to the static until Bela shouted at me to pack it in and I went to stare at myself in the bathroom mirror. I looked at my face a lot back then. Not because I thought I was pretty — I knew that I was not — but because eventually, if you stare long enough, you stop recognising yourself; you lose yourself. It's like if you say the same word over and over again — gradually it becomes just a sound. Meaningless. If you stare at yourself long enough you begin to look like someone else entirely or like no one at all. Sometimes I could pass half an hour like that, scaring myself witless with my own reflection.

My face and eyes are small and brown, the sockets dark like I've been punched. Two bruises that match the ones on my father's face. I have inherited his wounds. The backs of my hands, my knees and feet are also darker than the rest of me and like I've said, I've always cut my black hair short. In bright light, my arms look quite furry, like a spider's. I was small for my age and skinny. When I was thirteen I wore Push's hand-me-downs rather than my sisters', and strangers, if they thought about it at all, would assume I was a boy.

⋆ ⋆ ⋆

Later, when my sisters had come back drunk, and my dad had fallen asleep on the sofa and

Push had gone to bed, I lay awake and listened to Bela and Esha whispering in the dark. In the few weeks we had been here they had fallen in love with their new life. They were mad about London. They never talked about Leeds or their old friends, or Mum.

They threw themselves into trying out the pubs in Deptford and New Cross, starting college and planning their escape from our dad, our crappy house, and from me. They were sixteen and sick to death of death. They didn't want sadness anymore. Didn't want anything to bring them down. A soppy song on the radio? 'DePRESSing!' They'd switch stations. A tragic movie on the telly? 'BORing!' They'd kick Push to turn it over. Dad sitting in the dark, drinking beer? 'Just ignore him, silly old bat.' They weren't having any of it. Life was too short. Turn up the music, cheer up, have fun!

While I listened to them whisper I remembered how after Mum died I suddenly began to see her everywhere. Out of the corner of my eye I'd spot her in the strangest of places. As I wandered the streets when I should have been at school, a breathless laugh, a flash of red coat or a whiff of Anais-Anais would have me swivelling my head or snuffling up the air like a dog.

My mother had a lightness in her looks and

in herself that spilled into Push and the twins but that ran out by the time it was my turn. I, alone, was the dark dregs of my father's cup. And yet she loved us all and our house was a happy place, in its way. My dad, vague and quiet and usually to be found pottering with our beaten-up old Ford out front, or in our backyard's flower beds, she loved fiercely, protectively. If she'd find him sometimes staring into space or brooding somewhere by himself she'd bustle and boss him and kiss and hug him like she would with us and he'd blink into life with a surprised, delighted smile. Sometimes I'd catch them sitting together on the sofa or at the kitchen table, my mother laughing and the big, black bruises of my father's eyes holding her face in tender astonishment.

She was the life of our house, of us. The life, the glue, the point. Her broad Yorkshire accent, her wide lap, her laughter and her love would gently calm Push's restless energy, force my sisters to share their secret twin world with the rest of us, pull my father from his fuggy silences and forgive me, forgive me, stubbornly, determinedly, forgive me for being the person that I was.

And the rope that kept my family tethered was unbreakable, I thought. Strong. After she died I would often sneak into her wardrobe, just stand there in the dark among the coats

15

and dresses and fill myself with her smells. The perfume mingling with the sweet-sour smell of armpits and soap powder and that perfect smell that was just hers alone. But every time I returned the smell seemed to get a little less, like one of those scent-drenched strips you get in magazines that have been opened and discarded and left to fade. Eau de Mum. Until someone packed away her clothes when I was out one day. My mother was stacked neatly, violently, quietly, in boxes in our attic and that was that.

★　★　★

When my sisters finally fell asleep that night I knelt on my bed and lifted the nets to smoke one of their fags through the open window. I blew rings into the orange-tinged blackness for a while and then I saw Kyle come out of No. 33. He stood on his doorstep for a few seconds and I glanced at the radio-alarm clock. It was way past two. As I watched he knelt down to put on the shoes he'd been carrying, quietly closed the front door, then disappeared off down the street.

2

New Cross Hospital. 4 September 1986. Transcription of interview between Dr C Barton and Anita Naidu. Police copy.

Kyle's dead. They're all dead. I don't want to talk about it. I don't want to talk about it. I don't want to talk about it.

They think I'm strange no doubt, the people who live in this block. They're students, mostly. Of course I've changed my name since I was thirteen, and they don't recognise me as that little grim-faced girl with the black bar across her eyes in all the papers seven years ago. They don't recognise me in the way they would if it was Denis or Katie or Kyle (especially Kyle) who they passed in the hallway or on the stairs. For being alive — the sole 'survivor' — and still a child, I had the luxury of having my identity protected. No, my neighbours just see a skinny, short-haired boy-girl who has no visitors and won't return their smiles. In fact, except for Malcolm, I don't think I've ever said a word to a single other person living here.

I came here to Bristol not long after that summer. It was thought best, all things considered (I could hardly go back to Lewisham High, could I?). I was fostered out to a family up here, trained in dealing with people like me. And after I turned sixteen I got a factory job and just stayed.

Now and again I hear my name mentioned — my real name, I mean — and I freeze in shock. Whether it crops up in conversation with the girls in the factory, or there's a programme on TV, or the papers mention us in connection to some other case (James Bulger, for example), my reaction is always the same. A slow, creeping dread; the same sick fear that I'm going to be found out. Luckily the girls at the factory already think I'm odd, are used to my silence and my solitariness, and don't notice when I react like this.

When I first moved into this block of flats, my neighbours — the younger ones — tried to befriend me, taking me to be a student like them, I suppose. They'd bang on my door, ask to borrow a bottle-opener, invite me to their parties. It took them ages to understand I would never come. I watch them sometimes from my window when I cannot sleep, watch them returning from their raves and parties; hear them in the hallways boasting of the lads they've pulled, the girls they've had. I watch them stagger home at five, six, seven in the morning, their arms around each other's shoulders, and then I lie back on my bed and without even meaning to, I am back there, reliving that summer, wondering when it was, which particular point it might have been when I could perhaps have stopped what happened from happening.

*   *   *

The next day at school went pretty much the same as the first, with Denis cheerfully babbling away by my side. In the weeks that followed I grew used to having him about and even missed him when he went off to his special classes without me. He proudly told me that he had learning difficulties (no shit, I thought), and that it was in the special classes he'd first met Kyle (Kyle was different, he explained. Kyle had *behavioural* problems). And we'd see Kyle sometimes, sloping through the corridors by himself, sticking to the shadows, always staring at other people's feet. His hair was greasy, his uniform too long in the sleeves, too short in the legs. Skinny as a stick, he was the sort of kid you suspected would smell faintly of piss. The sort of kid nobody notices and you wouldn't remember if you had. Except I did, and I don't know why.

The same thing happened every afternoon. I'd walk out the gates with Denis then he'd sidle off to wait for Kyle, leaving me to go home on my own. But one day we were a little late coming out of class and Kyle was already there, waiting. This time I didn't let Denis shake me off and walked over to Kyle with him. He must have seen us coming but he kept looking at a spot just beyond us. For a while nobody spoke. Denis just stared down at his shoes as if he was about to get a bollocking off his mum. It was not going well.

'All right?' I said eventually. 'I'm Anita. I live opposite you.' Kyle stared hard at Denis, who muttered, 'She's in my class.'

Then Kyle nodded slowly and looked off down the street just waiting for me to go. I couldn't believe the nerve. These were two of the biggest losers in our school and even they didn't want to hang out with me. Still, I'm nothing if not persistent. 'Where you going then?' I said, like I wasn't bothered. 'Can I come?'

Finally he looked at me. His eyes were astonishing. A pale, flat grey, the colour of lampposts and gutters, the colour of rain, huge in his sharp, bony little face. Evidently he didn't like what he saw. With a jerk of his head to Denis, he moved suddenly off down the street, Denis trotting after him like a big fat awkward puppy. They didn't look back.

I stormed off to the bus thinking, wankers, wankers, wankers. Why did I mind so much? I wasn't after friends — had always preferred, actually, knocking about on my own. I bunked off a lot, wore the wrong kinds of clothes, had a boy's haircut and didn't give a fuck about Duran Duran. I didn't know what to say to the other kids nor they to me. They left me alone and that was only what I wanted.

I had got being ignored down to a fine art — and there is an art to it. It takes concentration and years of practice to ensure that you are constantly overlooked. I was a slipping-into-the-shadows sort of person, a disappearing-into-the-crowd sort of kid. Always on the periphery, a walking 'Do not disturb' sign. Nobody bothered me and I intended to keep it that way. I was the invisible girl. And yet. And yet. Something about Kyle tugged at me, pulled at me. I guess I must have seen something in him. I guess I saw me in him.

And at least Kyle and Denis looked like they had a purpose. They didn't seem to give a shit about school or the other kids either. I wanted to know where they were going, what they got up to after the last bell rang, where

21

Kyle went to at night. I just did. And I really wanted somewhere else to go other than back home.

Do I wish, now, that I'd kept away from them? Do I look back and curse the moment I first set eyes on Kyle? I just wish that he was still here. I miss him still, you see.

A few days later I got back to find Dad drinking tea with one of our neighbours. Janice was fortyish, ginger and fat, and each of her breasts was bigger than my head. Her make-up looked like she'd thrown it on with a bucket, and she wore the sort of clothes that looked good on my sisters, but kind of made you wince to see them on someone like her. My dad looked terrified, our neighbour's Lycra-clad rolls and ear-splitting laugh seemed to flatten him against the splashback like a dribble of spilt gravy. Next to her he appeared even more vague and hopeless than usual. In fact, I had never seen him so relieved to see me.

She spotted me before I had a chance to back out. 'You must be Anita!' she shrieked, thrilled. I started edging my way out the door, but Dad lassoed me with his panic.

'Anita, this is our neighbour, Janice.' He stood there nodding desperately, like some-one with Alzheimer's and clutching his can of Tennent's.

'Don't mind me, babes, come and sit down.' She beamed and patted the chair next to her. I sat in the one nearest the door. 'Thought I'd come and be neighbourly,' she said in the south-London whine I'd soon grow to hate. Her teeth were very small and yellow in her big, pink mouth. 'Been having a lovely chat with your dad,' she said. 'He's been telling me all about you.' I stared at my dad who started examining one of the buttons on his cardi.

Janice hugged her cup of tea to her cleavage, her piggy, mascara-clogged eyes suddenly brimming with compassion. 'Terrible what he's been through, bringing you all up on his own.' She looked at me like it was *my* fault Mum had dropped dead.

At last Janice cottoned on that I was the sort of silent, staring child who makes adults like her nervous and shut up. We both looked at my dad, who looked at his can. Luckily for Janice, at this point, Push came in.

My brother had never been one to shy away from a good cleavage and once the introductions had been made sat down with the air of a fifteen-year-old who has just found out he lives next door to Samantha Fox. 'I'll have to pop round for sugar sometime,' he said with a wink, and Janice giggled and patted her hair. Cocky, handsome, big-mouthed Push. Not for the first time Dad and I stared at him in amazement. Where did he come from? we silently asked each other.

After three minutes of Push banging on about himself, I was ready to make my escape. But I froze at the door when Janice said, 'Lewisham High, is it? So you must know that Kyle Kite.'

It was the first time I'd heard his full name but I knew instantly who she meant. Funny to think now, I suppose, how notorious that name has become, how synonymous it is with something I could barely comprehend back then. At the time though I merely turned back from the door, my curiosity pricked, to see her suck her cheeks in, raise her eyebrows and look at Dad as if to say 'WELL!'

'Kyle?' I asked, 'Kyle who lives opposite?'

'That's the one! No. 33.' She shook her head as if she was going to start welling up again. 'Such a sad business.'

'What was?' I wanted to strangle the words out of her.

'His little sister was Katie Kite!' She said the name triumphantly. Expectantly. Me, my dad and Push looked at each other, the penny almost but not quite dropping. The name vaguely but not really ringing a bell. We looked back at Janice, shaking our heads. Sorry, who?

'Little Katie Kite!' said Janice in exasperation. 'God almighty, don't you lot read the papers?'

Janice sighed and filled us in. One morning a year ago Kyle's mum ('nice lady, but a bit, you know . . . ') went to wake up little Katie, only she wasn't there. Five years old she was, gorgeous little thing. Vanished. No trace of her anywhere. 'Surely you remember? Front-page news!' We did, then. We remembered the headlines, the pictures of the little girl, the appeals for information. We remembered, but not clearly — our own nightmare was filling our thoughts back then.

'They never found her.' Janice cupped her tea closer. 'Just disappeared and nobody had a clue who did it.' She shuddered. 'Enough to drive anyone mad, wondering about it. Her mum never went out again. Poor Kyle does all their shopping. And his lovely granddad goes round too.'

Even Push was impressed. 'What, did someone have her away then?'

'That's just it, love. No one knows. The police were crawling around here for ages. No signs of a break-in. Couldn't find a thing. Total cock-up by the sounds of it. Hauling in half the neighbourhood, accusing all sorts. Even dragged the ex-husband back from God-knows-where but not a dicky bird. Poor little thing just disappeared and Christ only knows what became of her.'

Janice looked at each of our gaping faces with immense satisfaction and finished her tea.

⋆ ⋆ ⋆

The weeks before the end of term dragged on. Denis and I stuck together during the day and sometimes we'd catch glimpses of Kyle around school but he always ignored us. Often he'd turn up to meet Denis after he'd clearly been bunking off all day. I'd managed to break Denis's habit of answering my every question with his own retarded ones, but on the subject of Kyle he was unforthcoming. It was mind-bendingly frustrating. If I'd been interested in Kyle before, now I was fascinated. Imagine knowing someone whose sister had vanished?

I once asked Denis if he ever went round to Kyle's. He looked a bit shifty and tried to turn the conversation back to dinosaurs or Curly Wurlys or whatever the fuck he'd been talking about. But after I went on at him he said, 'Yeh, well no, not really. Mostly we go out and do stuff.'

I asked him what sort of stuff.

'Just mucking about sort of stuff. Down by the river.'

I looked at him with my 'Don't be a dickhead' face.

'Looking for caves,' he said.

Caves? Looking for what caves? But Denis escaped into his sodding Home Economics class to learn how to make shepherd's pie, and that was that.

★ ★ ★

The days slouched on, dragging their heels towards the end of term, each one much like the last until suddenly one morning something a bit weird happened. By then I'd got into the swing of things at Lewisham High. My teachers were so relieved that I was the sort of kid who kept her head down and her mouth shut that they pretty much left me to my own devices. That particular day I was in Maths with Denis. We were both in the bottom class — him for obvious reasons, me because it was easier to play dumb and coast along with the retards rather than have to get involved and take part with the few kids in that place who actually gave a shit. The teachers were far too busy trying to keep World War III from breaking out to bother with the likes of me.

So after Maths, Denis and I came out of our classroom to find Kyle right outside. He was just standing there in the corridor really still, his fists clenched, his eyes on the floor, but he was doing this thing, the thing I do too, of pretending that he wasn't really there. I recognised it straightaway, that haziness; the inaccuracy of him, like, even though you were looking directly at him, it was really like you were only seeing him from the corner of your eye. Shadowy. There's a certain knack to that.

He was with three other kids and they were taking the piss out of him, laughing at him, and he had his back to the wall like he was trying to blend into it. They were saying stuff like, 'Fucking tramp', that sort of thing. 'Weirdo.' Just the sort of thing kids like us got all the time. You just ignored it. But then one of them, a tall lanky girl said, 'Where's your kid sister then?' and she started laughing, you know that Ahahahahahaha high-pitched sort of fake laughing kids do when they know they're not really being funny.

That's when it happened. Kyle looked up then, straight at the girl who had said it, and it was like suddenly all of him that he'd been hiding, pretending wasn't there, zoomed back into him with such brute force that all of him and his anger and hatred for those kids suddenly concentrated, focused into his eyes with the speed of a bullet. And the girl stopped laughing like she'd been slapped.

Her face just dropped, just went completely blank with shock. Then Kyle went for her, just sort of lunged at her. And she ran, then. She ran as fast as she could but Kyle just threw himself off down the corridor after her.

By this time a bit of a crowd had gathered so we all chased after them, the other kids yelling, 'Fight! Fight! Fight!' We chased them down the corridors and up the stairs and when we reached the top there they were: Kyle and the girl. He had her by the throat. She was half-bent backwards over the banister, half-hanging over the stairwell — quite high up they were, Kyle's thumbs pressed into her windpipe, her eyes all bulging and red. All the other kids just went really quiet.

A teacher came and broke it up, yanked Kyle by the elbow away from the girl and marched him off to the headmaster's office and that was that. And I remember thinking then that I would do practically anything to be friends with Kyle.

★   ★   ★

Suddenly it was the end of term. Seven whole weeks with no school stretching ahead of me and I didn't have a thing to do. Some mornings I'd just sit on our steps in the

29

sunshine, watching the people go by. Push got a summer job and my sisters hung out in the nearby park with their new college mates, taking it in turns to buy cider and fags. Sometimes I'd see Denis come and knock for Kyle. He'd turn and wave at me if he saw me hanging about, but Kyle never looked back when they went off down the street together. Occasionally I'd see an old man letting himself into No. 33, but I never saw any sign of Kyle's mum. I tried to imagine what their house was like inside, but the curtains were always drawn and I could only picture dark empty rooms behind them.

The day that everything changed was a Saturday. I was bored shitless of hanging around the house while Dad watched cartoons so I decided to go into Lewisham.

The streets of our bit of Brockley were wide and long with tall skinny houses that felt like they were leaning forward, like they were about to fall down on you with their pointy roofs and their big bay windows like gaping mouths. The pavements were lined with trees so big their roots had started to push up through the tarmac like trapped arms. I tripped over them a hundred times in those first few weeks.

I walked until I got to the hill that goes down to Lewisham, the slopes of Crystal

Palace and Forest Hill behind me, Deptford and Greenwich spread out below. You could see the masts of the *Cutty Sark* from there, the river twisting behind it. Buses thundered past me as I walked down the hill. Soul music blasted from open doors and the primary-coloured Caribbean shop fronts jingle-jangled in the dust between the crumbly bricked houses, black and white stickers peeling off their dirty windows that said 'CND' and 'Ban The Bomb'. I kept my eyes on my flip-flops as they picked their way along the dips and hollows of the dried-up pavements.

Packed, Lewisham was. When I reached the high street I was overwhelmed suddenly by the mobs of Saturday morning shoppers; teenagers with pushchairs, tramps with their cans, religious nuts shouting into loud speakers, cars blaring music. A 180 bus stopped and not caring where it was going, I got on.

It wasn't until I'd sat down on the top deck that I realised Kyle and Denis were sitting on the seat across from me. They didn't notice me at first. Kyle was sitting neat and compact, his scrawny white neck rigid as he stared at a fat girl eating a burger in front of him. Denis, taking up most of the seat, was jiggling his knees up and down, whistling the same long thin note between his teeth. I watched Kyle watch the fat girl, noticed his disgust at the way she gnawed at her food, fat globs of mayonnaise and relish dripping onto her hands. The bus chugged, unbearably hot, towards Greenwich.

Then, suddenly, from the smoke-fogged seats at the back came, 'There's those fucking gypos from school.'

Kyle kept looking straight ahead, but Denis and I both turned, our eyes meeting briefly, knowing instantly what this meant. At the back of the bus sat Mike Hunt and his mates Lee and Marco. I had been at Lewisham High long enough to know that this was seriously bad news. I was surprised they'd had time to notice Kyle and Denis long enough to recognise them, busy as they usually were setting fire to each other or getting shitfaced on glue in the toilets. They were in my brother's year, and they were grade-A psychos. Mike was so hard nobody even ever took the piss out of him for having a name that basically sounded like 'my cunt'. His older brother was in prison for stabbing some bloke and you got the feeling Mike wasn't far behind him. It was said he'd been expelled from his last school for sexually assaulting one of his teachers. Most of the time Mike and his friends were in Lewisham High's off-site and optimistically titled

'Improvement Centre', but otherwise they terrorised the corridors and playing fields, looking for someone's day to ruin. And they were making their way towards us.

The fat girl got up and Mike and Marco fell into her empty seat, Lee next to me. Mike was so blond and pale you could see the veins of his face behind his thin white skin. 'What's this then?' he said. 'Spastics' day out?'

Denis looked anxiously at Kyle.

'Oi!' Mike's voice was suddenly so loud every passenger on the packed bus swivelled their heads towards him. 'I asked you a fucking question.' His laugh was ear-splitting, shrill as a girl's. 'You seen what they're wearing?' he asked Lee. Marco, his face grey and greasy as uncooked hamburger, spat dismissively at Denis's head. Conversation from the other passengers petered out.

I saw Denis glance down guiltily at his and Kyle's outfits. He was wearing a too-small T-shirt with a picture of Inspector Clouseau on the front, the words, 'Where's that rinky-dink panther?' written in curly pink writing underneath. Kyle was dressed with his customary disregard for either fashion or temperature in tweed trousers two sizes too big and a nasty brown nylon jumper. His bony elbows poked through little holes in the sleeves. To be fair they did look like a couple of gypos. But Kyle was still looking straight ahead, as if he hadn't noticed them yet.

Marco turned to Mike and pointed proudly at his top. 'Kappa, this is. Thirty-eight quid right? My dad got it from this shop up West, yeh?'

Mike snorted. 'Fucking shit that is.' He pointed at his lime-green sweatshirt. 'Lacoste. Forty-three quid down Romford, so fuck off.' They turned their attention back to Kyle and Denis. 'Where you going then, girls?'

Kyle sighed, stood up, and with a flick of his head to Denis, signalled for him to get up too. A sudden recklessness made me slip past Lee to join them. The three lads got up to bar our way. 'Off somewhere, wanker?' Marco asked Kyle softly. Mike noticed me for the first time. 'All right, Paki. Want some too do you?' He turned to his mates and laughed. 'Seen the state of these cunts?'

Lee shoved his face in Denis's. 'Give us a fiver and you can go.' Denis looked like he was going to shit himself.

When Kyle finally spoke, it was with the gravely sympathetic air of a doctor imparting very bad news. 'Mike,' he began sadly, as the other passengers craned forward to listen. 'Your mum's a lesbian, your sister's on the game and your dad sucks cock. Now let me off the fucking bus. Please.'

There was a moment of silence, then an eruption of shocked laughter from a crowd of black kids at the front and suddenly the rest of the bus were shaking their heads and smiling in disbelief too. Mike looked like someone had thrown a brick in his face. 'Hah?' he said.

One of the black kids shouted, 'Let them off the fucking bus, batty-boy.'

A fat girl with braids got up and made shooing motions with her hand. 'Get out of the man's way, you pasty little shit.' Her boyfriend, big and menacing, kissed his teeth at Mike. 'Let them through, man, or shall I kick ya bony ass?' His friends started laughing, waving their right hands till their fingers clicked, shouting 'Shaaaaaaaaame!' and 'Buuuuuuuuuurn!' while the girl, creasing up, said, 'Bwoy! Mama's a lesbian!' She wiped pretend tears from her eyes and shook her head slowly. 'Oh my gosh, that's harsh, man.'

Mike's only option was to feign indifference. Shrugging, he moved aside to let us pass. Me and Denis followed Kyle downstairs. The bus kept level with us for a while as we walked in silence. As it finally veered off to the right, a window slid open and Mike's face appeared in the little square gap. He gobbed at each of us, three wet balls of spit landing expertly on our heads.

3

We make telephones at the factory where I work. I've been there for four years. Every day for four years I have been responsible for sticking the manufacturer's logo onto the bottom of the handset. Millions and millions of sticky labels I have attached, each one identical to the last. I am a good worker, Doctor Barton. I am quiet, steady and fast and I always beat my targets. At first the other workers resented me for it, but once they realised I was oblivious to their remarks and dirty looks they gave up and now I am to them like part of the bench I sit on every day.

And the days and weeks dissolve into each other, they dissolve. I measure out each one carefully, inch by inch, fraction by fraction, until it is night and I can go home and wait for Malcolm.

Malcolm is nineteen, six months younger than me, and he lives with his mum in my block. He washes up in the kitchen of a Mexican restaurant called Speedy Gonzales. I knew there was something different about him right away. I mean, I knew there was something different about how I felt about him. I wasn't afraid of him. I didn't want to duck my head and run into my bedsit whenever I passed him. I usually avoid people's eyes and so does he, but after I had been here for a year we just gently, bit by bit, started letting ourselves *not* look away, whenever we passed on the stairs or in the corridor. We didn't smile or anything, didn't speak, but we started to let our eyes rest awhile on each other's. Which is a lot, an awful lot, for people like me and Malcolm.

★　★　★

Denis, Kyle and I had got off the bus in the middle of Greenwich, the market place and cafes spewing tourists come to buy cheap antiques or second-hand jeans. We started walking towards the river and the high masts of the *Cutty Sark*. When we reached the boat I stopped. Denis looked at me questioningly. 'You coming then?'

I glanced at Kyle, who was squinting up at the sun and fiddling with a cigarette butt he'd pulled from his pocket. He shrugged and nodded. The three of us walked on.

The day had the kind of hyper-real, orange-hued brightness that engraves itself in memories, the sky so blue I felt I could reach up and tear chunks from it. At the river we stopped to watch some tourists get on the pleasure boat. A woman handed out ice creams to her kids as her husband took pictures from the jetty. Kyle stared across the river at the scrappy brown wastelands of the Isle of Dogs then looked pointedly at the brick and glass-domed entrance to the Thames' foot tunnel. Denis shook his head. 'I'm not going down there,' he said. It was clearly a familiar request. He shuddered and turned to me. 'Don't like being underground.' Kyle shrugged and we turned towards the cool shaded walkway that follows the Thames' bank in the direction of Woolwich.

We fell into single file, Kyle leading the way. We didn't speak, each of us dragging a hand along the black iron railings, our faces turned towards the river, scenting out like dogs the water's warm, yeasty whiff as it lapped gently below. To our right was the cold white stone of the Royal Naval College, looming and magnificent in the midday heat.

On we walked, past laughing, beery pubs, down cobbled lanes then out again to the deserted narrow streets of east Greenwich. We were alone suddenly, no tourists or weekend shoppers there. Just little rows of black-bricked houses in the shadow of an enormous power station in a perpetual sullen stand-off. Tiny pubs on corners, an air of recent violent brawls, in the dark cracks we glimpsed lone old men with fag-butts for fingers staring at their pints.

We joined the river again and made our way to the grassy wastelands that scorched and browned between some warehouses. On a steel girder in an empty boat-yard we smoked the cigarettes I'd stolen from my sisters' stash. The air was thick with river smells and hazy with heat. Distant clankings from the scrapyards mixed with shouts of laughter from a nearby beer garden while the Thames lapped below us like the sea-shore. A whiff of molasses from the animal feed factory drifted and mingled with the sounds and light like liquid, the sun scorching the tops of our heads and the backs of our hands. I watched the river turn and tug and thought that somewhere it must join up with the sea, somewhere very far away I'd never been.

'Did you know,' said Kyle eventually, 'that if two people were to hold hands for like, years and years and years, never letting go I mean — like eating and going to school and that, just holding hands all the time — that their skin would eventually grow over each other's and they'd be joined up?'

Denis gazed at him with silent respect for a

while before eventually asking, 'What if they weren't in the same class, though?'

★ ★ ★

Seven years have passed since that summer. Here in my little room in Bristol I look out over the quiet Clifton streets and the distant fields and hills, but what I see are the banks of the river Thames. That day was the start of it all, see — the start of me, Denis and Kyle. And despite everything, despite what was to come, I smile when I think of the three of us then. The truth is, those first few weeks we spent together were the best of my life. You look a little shocked, Doctor Barton. But just listen. Listen to me.

★ ★ ★

That first day Kyle and I didn't talk much. The few times I did speak to him it was like dropping a stone down a very deep well. He'd look at me with vacant eyes until whatever I'd said finally hit the bottom of him and you could almost hear the 'plop', then he'd blink and either answer, or not. Mostly I kept quiet as we smoked and listened to one of Denis's rambling stories and threw sticks in to the river, but my eyes kept returning to Kyle's

40

face; that guarded, always-thinking face like one of those rodenty, bug-eyed cats. But his eyes were as grey as stones, as grey as the river. A face that could utterly shock you with its rare half-smiles like a sudden crack of light in a dark room.

I got the feeling that he wasn't mad keen on me being there, and while he was used to Denis's constant chatter and questions, I was merely being put up with for that one brief day.

'Are we going to look for caves?' Denis asked Kyle when we'd been sitting there a while. The look Kyle shot back said it all. I was not to be trusted.

★   ★   ★

We watched boats pass; flash yuppies' speed boats, the slow glide of the rowers' club and once a police boat ripping through the grey stillness, scattering swans and driftwood and the gently bobbing plastic bottles. To our right the mangled iron mountains of the scrap heaps loomed pink and blue in front of a gaggle of orange cranes. As the sun started to sink, we trailed slowly back along the river, walking in silence through the backstreets of Greenwich.

Kyle saw them first.

I had become lost in watching my feet walk, hypnotised by the steady pace of my flip-flops: one-two-left-right-click-clack-flip-flop, and hadn't noticed that Kyle had stopped until I was nearly on his heels. I looked up when I heard Denis whimper in panic. When I followed Kyle's gaze I thought, simply, 'They're going to kick our heads in,' and I felt the blood rush to my ears.

Mike, Lee and Marco were about 100 yards away, and had been joined by four other lads. They were outside a shop at the end of the street, kicking empty beer cans at each other or leaning on cars, boredom and cigarette smoke rising from their huddle into the darkening sky. We were too far down the street now to turn back unnoticed and without saying a word Kyle grabbed Denis's arm and we started pegging it back the way we came. As we ran we heard Mike shouting out ecstatically to his mates.

Back at the boat-yard we ducked down behind a low wall. We heard seven pairs of Nikes slapping on tarmac then come to a stop just metres from where we hid. Seconds dripped by like years. I looked at Denis, goggle-eyed and quivering beside me. He reminded me of a beaten dog crouched miserably there, waiting to be told what to do. 'Let's go to our *place*, Kyle,' he said desperately. 'We could hide there.'

But Kyle held up his hand to silence him. The lads were arguing about where we could have gone and Kyle pointed to a gap in some railings fifty yards away. 'Those steps go down to the river,' his whisper was barely more than a wheeze. 'If the tide is out, we can cut along the edge and back to Greenwich.'

Denis and I nodded. We heard the lads move off to check out the parking lot opposite. The three of us, keeping low behind the wall, made a break for the steps. Just as we reached them we heard Mike shout out. We had been seen.

We almost free-fell down those steps, skidding and slipping on the slimy moss. I prayed please God, please God, please God, let the tide be out now. At the bottom there was about two feet of silty, green muck to run along, the stinking river nibbling at our feet. I could barely see or hear now, and just ran blindly after Kyle. My head started to throb with the effort of running, and I felt each footfall like a punch in the throat. I looked over my shoulder. Denis, his chin jutting out, his eyes white and his lips pulled back, was flailing along like a demented elephant a few metres back. Behind him the lads were almost sauntering down the steps.

Finally we saw the next set of stairs ahead. With one more spurt of effort I caught up with Kyle and together we climbed the dank, green stone. We turned to look for Denis. 'Den, for fuck's sake, come on,' Kyle shouted. 'Come ON!'

Whimpering and gasping, his eyes on Kyle, Denis finally made it to the top.

Once up on the walkway we steamed our way through the tourists and at last rounded the corner to the *Cutty Sark*. We had, probably, twenty seconds left of being completely out of Mike's sight. There was nowhere for us to hide in that open space. Kyle looked towards the entrance to the foot tunnel. So out of breath he could barely speak, he gripped Denis by the elbow. 'Look. Den. We. Have. To. Go. Down. There.'

Panic-stricken, Denis looked from Kyle, to the tunnel's entrance, to the corner where he knew Mike and the others were going to appear any second. 'I can't, Kyle. I just can't. I don't want to.'

'Denis, listen to me. They're going to kick our heads in. Come. Fucking. On.' Then Kyle ran towards the red and glass dome. A split second later me and Denis followed him.

To get down to the foot tunnel you can

either walk down a load of spiral steps or take an ancient, creaky lift. We made the lift just as the operator slid the metal doors closed. Falling inside the wood-panelled cube, we let it slowly drop us below the Thames, the blue-uniformed man and a couple of German tourists watching us nonplussed as we gasped bug-eyed on the bench.

I don't know if you've ever been down the Greenwich foot tunnel, but it's a pretty spooky place. You feel like you're in the icy, slimy intestines of an enormous snake. When you get out of the lift the temperature drops twenty degrees, and the tunnel dips away from you, the end nowhere in sight. The Thames drips through the roof into dank puddles that glimmer and flicker in the yellow light. It's on a slight slant and once you start running you can't seem to stop, but the craziest thing are the echoes; every noise returning amplified and monstrous to smack you in the face. We legged it through the tunnel until we got to the middle, the sounds of our footsteps bouncing off the tiles. Finally we slowed to a halt. We had lost them. There was no way Mike could catch us now. I laughed and clapped my hands, and it sounded like thunder down there. Even Kyle let out a short, sharp bark of pleasure. Denis, his head down and fists clenched with fear, saved his relief until we were safely out the other side.

But we had escaped Mike, and we had done it together, and I felt that it somehow meant something. That it meant I was a part of things then.

There's no way back to Greenwich from the Isle of Dogs other than that tunnel. It took us ages to get home. As we wandered through those wasted docklands, that no-man's land of lonely estates and random forgotten terraces, we could see signs of the regeneration, the glory that was to come. A lone digger, a crane, an air of quiet flux and expectation. Like a battered housewife who's suddenly been promised the stars but has been beaten down too much to believe it. Yet still an air of grudging hope. A place wanting to believe it was on the brink of something big. Like we were, like we were.

We finally found a bus to take us home and Denis and I went over and over what had happened, laughing at our cunning and luck. We shared a fag at the back of the top deck, each taking a puff then passing it on, our feet hanging over the seats in front of us. I will always remember that bus ride, how happy I felt just to be there with them.

Eventually Denis turned to look admiringly at Kyle. 'I can't believe you told Mike his dad sucks cock,' he said, his voice hushed with awe. Kyle shrugged and looked out the window, but he definitely smiled.

When Denis got off a couple of stops before us, he waved from the stairs and said, 'See you later, yeh?' and me and Kyle nodded, and said, 'Yeh.'

But as we made our way up Myre Street a silence fell between us. Suddenly Kyle's face was tight and closed again, his head bent almost to his chest, and when we got to my house he barely seemed to notice when I said goodbye. I watched from my step as he walked up to his front door, saw how his scrawny shoulder blades tightened under his thin jumper. As he stood there a man with white hair appeared and after saying a few words, ushered him in, the heavy front door slamming closed behind them, the light in their hall snapping instantly off.

4

New Cross Hospital. 4 September 1986.
Transcription of interview between Dr C
Barton and Anita Naidu. Police copy.

*He shut me down there with them, pulled the
boards and the girders across so I couldn't
get out. I don't know why he did that. Why
would he do that? Why would he keep me
down there with the other two dead? They're
saying he was a psycho, that's what the police
are all saying but he was my best friend. I sat
there for hours. I had my arms wrapped
around my knees and my eyes closed tight
because I didn't want to see how black it was
and I didn't want to touch anything or
anything to touch me. And I didn't know
what was worse, the whole time I was down
there, I couldn't make up my mind which
would be worse: being left down there, or
him coming back.*

By eight o'clock the next morning I was up,
dressed, and staring out the window like a
dog needing a walk. Had Denis said 'See you
tomorrow' when he got off the bus last night?

Or had it just been 'See you later'? Had he meant that he'd be seeing both of us later, or just Kyle? What if yesterday had been a one-off? Eventually I left my spot behind the front-room curtains and wandered irritably back upstairs.

My sisters were lying in bed, chatting about the night before. Esha, a cigarette in one hand, a can of Coke in the other, was blowing smoke rings at the ceiling while Bela painted her toenails pink. They both had yesterday's eyeliner on their cheeks and matching Care Bears on their pillows and they were deep in conversation.

Esha was saying, 'So then he goes to me, 'Was your mum and dad retarded?''

Bela looked up from her foot. 'Cheeky git! Why'd he want to know that?'

'That's what I said,' replied Esha. 'So he goes, 'Cos, my sweetheart, there's something really special about you!''

Bela cocked her head for a moment to consider this, the nail varnish brush poised in mid air. 'Aw! So what did you say?'

'I said, 'In that case I'll have a Martini and lemonade, ta very much.'' My sisters both cackled appreciatively.

'So then,' Esha shot me a glance and lowered her voice. 'So then he goes, 'Do you want to come outside and look at my motor?''

'Nah!'

'Yeh! So I goes, 'Not bloody likely, you're old enough to be my dad, you!''

'As if!' agreed Bela.

Esha stared thoughtfully at her cigarette for a moment. 'But I did, like. In the end.'

'Yeh,' said Bela, squinting at her toes.

'Well,' said Esha. 'He *had* bought me six Martinis and lemonades after all.'

'Aw,' said Bela. 'Well, that's nice then, innit?'

'For God's sake, Nit,' Esha suddenly shouted. 'Will you please just pack that in?'

'Pack what in?' I asked, continuing to bash out the 'Match Of The Day' theme tune on the window with a cigarette lighter.

'That!' She threw her pillow at my head and I went back downstairs.

The possibility of seven empty weeks filled with bollocksall to do finally forced me first onto our front step and then to the kerb outside No. 33, where I sat with my feet between two parked cars, looking down the street for Denis.

Two hours later and I was still there. I had brought Push's PacMan out with me and eventually became so caught up in beating his highest score that I didn't even hear the door behind me open. I looked up to see the old man from the night before staring down at

50

me, Kyle hovering just behind him and clearly not thrilled to see me sat there, like a fag butt in the gutter.

'Hello,' I said.

Kyle nodded briefly. The old man was staring at me in surprise. 'Hello, dear,' he said. 'Was it Kyle you were waiting for?' His voice was gentle, a bit Scottish or something. He was buttoned up in a smart tweed jacket as if he was going somewhere special.

I shrugged and looked at Kyle. 'You and Denis coming out today?'

Kyle barely glanced at me. 'Nah,' he said.

'Oh,' I said. 'Right.'

I looked up at Kyle's granddad who was smiling now like something was funny. But he had a nice face. I looked at his white, bushy brows for a bit. Finally, to fill the silence, I said, 'I'm Anita.'

I saw Kyle roll his eyes. The old man held out his hand. 'Very nice to meet you, Anita. I'm Patrick.'

'I live opposite,' I muttered, jerking my head towards the other side of the road. The old man nodded and looked politely across at our tatty little house, put there to fill a hole a bomb had left once, the bins spilling beer cans and Kentucky Fried Chicken boxes onto our steps. I blushed, aware of how crappy it looked compared to theirs and the other big old-fashioned ones in the street.

'I see,' he said. 'And were you waiting for my grandson here?'

I looked at Kyle and said pathetically, 'Wondered what you and Denis were doing today.'

Kyle glanced at me. An expression in his eyes that made the hopeful feeling that had been bobbing around behind my ribs all morning sink to my feet and seep out of my toenails.

'It's Sunday,' he told me. 'Denis will be at church.' I didn't know what to say to that. Denis was a God-botherer? It was news to me.

The old man said, 'Well now,' and, doing a little bow like old gents do in films, put his hand on Kyle's shoulder and they walked off down the street. Great, I thought. Fanfuck-ingtastic. 'Bollocks,' I said to no one, to myself.

★ ★ ★

That night I lay awake listening to our neighbours arguing. A steady crescendo of pissed-up rage from the burly, beardy bloke from No. 34, his stringy, mean-eyed wife bitch-ing, goading, crowing, their voices entwining to seep through our flimsy walls, bubbling behind our wallpaper like water from a leaky pipe until at last a sudden bellow, a crash, then silence. I got up to smoke a cigarette.

Sticking my head out of the bedroom window I watched the foxes and drunks weave and stagger up Myre Street. At half-one I saw Kyle creep out of his front door then slope off into the night again. 'Where do you go?' I asked him silently. 'Where do you go to at night?'

I smoked my cigarette and thought about Katie Kite. I pictured a little blonde girl with Kyle's big grey eyes and wondered who had taken her and where. I gazed at the still, dark house opposite and tried to imagine what had happened there a year ago. I wondered if she was dead or not, and whether the person who broke into people's houses to snatch kids would be coming back to Myre Street any time soon. Eventually I threw the fag butt out the window, lay back down on my bed, and tried not to think about anything at all.

★ ★ ★

A few empty, tedious days passed. There was no sign of Kyle or Denis and my family were driving me round the bend. When Push was in, he was as bored as I was and if we ever found ourselves in the same room together it was only a matter of minutes before we wanted to rip each other's throats out. Dad was either parked in front of the telly with his beer, or he was listening to Janice talk bollocks in the kitchen.

One morning when Push was out I wandered into his bedroom to look for his PacMan. Esha and Bela were still in bed, watching telly on the black and white next door. I liked it in Push's room, its cool blue walls and uncluttered calm were lovely to me after the stuffy, hairspray-stinking chaos of our bedroom. His room didn't get the sun like ours did, and I lay back on his bed in the chilly stillness, idly listening to the telly next door and Janice shrieking with laughter in the kitchen below (she had to be the only person alive who still found my dad that amusing). I was enjoying the fact that Push would go spastic if he knew I was in there. I rolled on my side to face the open window, and felt something hard beneath the duvet.

I'd seen porn mags before of course, on the top shelves in shops, but this was the first time I'd ever looked inside one. There was no one there to see me but still I felt my cheeks burn as I leafed through its pages. I stared at the centre spread of three women, their breasts enormous, their legs spread, their expressions varying from comatosed to surprised.

'What the fuck do you think you're doing?'

I jumped to my feet and the magazine fell onto the floor, flopping open to a picture of a girl sucking her own nipple, her fingers spreading herself down below. Push was standing in the doorframe, his green eyes cold and furious.

'Nothing,' I said. 'I — ' Push looked from me to the magazine and sprinted across the room. 'You little bitch,' he said. 'You dirty little bitch! Having a good look, were you?' His face was red with shame.

'I was looking for the PacMan,' I said feebly. I couldn't look at him and felt almost as if it was I who was naked in the pictures of the magazine.

I can see now how it must have been for Push back then. Not easy to get laid when you looked like him. All those blonde, big-titted Lewisham High girls who wouldn't be seen dead going out with 'an Asian', how they'd kick themselves now if they could see the man he was to grow into — if they could see the beauty that was to come. But there in that room I didn't think any of that, of course. I was innocent for my age I except, but those pictures were a smack in the face; a rude awakening.

'Leave me alone,' I said. 'I wasn't doing anything.'

'Keep the fuck out of my room,' he ranted. 'Look at you. Dressed like a bloke and staring at girls' knockers. You a fucking lezzer or what?' And suddenly my left ear was ringing and burning where he'd slapped it. We stared at each other for a couple of seconds then I ran from the room, down the stairs and out the front door, where I fell smack bang into Denis who was about to ring the bell.

Denis trotted beside me while I gradually calmed down. Out of the corner of my eye I could see his flab jump about. Eventually we stopped at a railway bridge and hung over the wall, looking down at the train tracks below us. The bridge was covered in graffiti and I recognised one of the tags. I'd seen that same word sprayed in various colours and sizes on every wall, lamppost and bridge in south-east London. 'Enrol', it said, and whoever he was he'd been a busy lad. As I stood there with Denis I found myself wondering about this Enrol person; why he felt the need to announce himself like that in foot-high letters wherever he went. Maybe he just wanted to prove he was there, I thought. Show the world he existed. As I stood there that morning looking at his name repeated fifty times on the bricks, I thought that that was a strange thing to want to do. But I wonder what ever happened to him? I wonder where he is now? I guess his plan worked: I didn't forget him, did I?

'You seen Kyle?' asked Denis eventually.

I turned to look at him and felt my mood lift a bit. It was good to see him even if he did stink of BO that day. 'Nah,' I said.

He pulled a Mars bar from his pocket and began to munch. 'Me neither.'

We walked on, towards Deptford.

'Where do you think he is?' I asked.

'Dunno,' said Denis. 'He said something about going to Point Hill.'

I didn't know where Point Hill was, and didn't much care if we found Kyle or not. It was just good to be out of the house and going somewhere. Denis started telling me a long and complicated story about his Uncle Richard who lived in Broadstairs and had once met Big Daddy and we got on the bus up to Blackheath. From there we walked over the common towards Greenwich Park but instead of heading towards the donkey rides and ice cream vans, Denis led me to a little side park — a field at the top of Blackheath Hill from which you could see all of London stretched out below. Denis pointed to someone sitting on a bench. Kyle.

When we reached him he didn't seem

particularly surprised to see us and barely glanced up. He looked tired, his eyes dull and sunken in his scrawny face. We sat in silence for a while, listening to Denis get his breath back and looking down on the city below us. The river flickered green and silver through the mangled, scrambled, silent mess of streets and parks and cranes and buildings, a billion windows blinking back up at us. Denis went off to buy ice lollies and we lay on our fronts on the scratchy yellow grass to eat them.

'There's a cave underneath this hill,' said Kyle, finally.

'I know,' said Denis, sucking the big toe off his Funny Foot.

'I wasn't talking to you,' said Kyle.

A sharp bite of pleasure. 'A cave?' I said.

'It's called Jack Cade's Cavern.' He began carefully squashing ants with his lolly stick.

I listened to Kyle talk, his face so animated suddenly he almost looked like a kid. He told me about the tunnels and caves beneath Greenwich. Chalk mines, some of them, the biggest one right beneath our bellies. Now long closed up, Kyle said it had been where smugglers stashed their loot two hundred years ago. 'No one knows where the entrance is, though. I've looked, I've looked all round this hill hundreds of times but it's all just grass now.'

We ate our ice lollies in silence for a bit. Then Kyle said, 'There are others, further into Greenwich; old sand mines and secret bunkers from the war, and some people reckon there are smugglers' tunnels by the river and then of course there are the chalk mines under Blackheath and the water conduits in the park.'

I could barely believe it was the same Kyle, his pale, usually flat grey eyes were actually shining.

'I've read all about them,' he said. His voice became lower and he looked at me carefully. I scarcely breathed. 'And I reckon there are more. Sand mines and that. There must be. Secret places that no one's found yet.'

'But Kyle's gonna find them!' said Denis, proudly. 'And he's gonna live in one, just like Seany Bean!'

'Seany who?' I asked.

'He was this bloke in Scotland who lived in a cave with his family and they'd set traps for people and rob them and take them back to the cave and eat them!'

'Oh,' I said.

'Shut up, Denis,' said Kyle.

★   ★   ★

Eventually we got up and walked to Greenwich. The day burned and glittered and

59

on the way down the hill I said, 'Your granddad seems all right.' Kyle looked at me then quickly away again. 'He live with you then?' I asked.

Kyle shook his head. 'He just comes at weekends, and he's staying for the summer holidays to look after me.'

'Oh,' I said. 'That's nice.'

Ahead of us a rare breeze was causing a shower of pinky-white petals to fall from a blossom tree and Denis was staring at it transfixed. 'It's snowing!' he grinned. We went and stood underneath the tree, raising our faces to the falling flowers. Denis started heaping together petals from the ground and throwing them in the air and at me, and I laughed and threw them back at him. Kyle stood watching us for a while, before shrugging and walking on.

We made our way to East Greenwich, ducking in and out of warm bricked alleys that smelt of baked dust and yeast, brief and secretive respites from the burning sun. We cut through hostile, empty, little streets then trudged through aimless wasteland, the river always nudging, edging, pushing somewhere below like a cat circling your ankles.

We got to the shore and hung over the railings to watch the people with metal detectors hoover the beach below us. 'Look,' I said, spotting a family of ducklings. Kyle picked up a stick and threw it at them. 'Don't,' I said before I could stop myself, as the ducklings scattered for safety.

'There's still one there,' said Denis, peering between the railings. On the beach one of the parent ducks was struggling to get up. Every time it staggered to its feet it fell back again. We watched for a while. 'Think it's dying,' said Denis.

Kyle was scrabbling about in the flowerbed behind us. He came back armed with pebbles and small rocks. We watched as he aimed them one by one at the duck's head. The duck flopped its long neck and its head fell back onto the beach. It seemed to give up. 'No, don't,' I said again.

But Kyle didn't seem to hear me. He jumped over the railings onto the beach. Denis and I looked at each other before following him. Kyle was crouched down by the duck with a large rock in his hand. It was still alive, its eyes staring up at Kyle, its beak working but no sound coming out. Half-heartedly it flapped its wings. Before either me or Denis could say anything, Kyle smashed the rock into the duck's head, bashing it again and again until it was pulp, and bits of brain and beak and eyes and feathers were stuck to Kyle's rock. Denis went and sat on a step until it was over. And still Kyle kept bashing it, like it was just another stone, long after it was clearly fucking dead.

Eventually he got up, blinking in surprise at my repulsed face. 'What?' he asked. When I didn't reply he shrugged and said, 'I was doing it a favour,' and without a word we walked to the bus stop, leaving the annihilated bird where it was. Kyle behaved as if nothing at all had happened, Denis ate some Wotsits. And me? I ignored the sick feeling in my stomach.

★   ★   ★

We spent nearly every day of that summer by the river. We loved it. Even when we ventured up to the park or the heath we'd keep it in our sight, as if we couldn't quite bear to leave it completely — and sooner or later we'd always end up by its banks again. But every time we returned, it was like an entirely different river to the one we'd left. Sometimes the water had shrivelled away to reveal the naked, oily wreckage of its shores. Or the water would be so high it licked at our shoes as we stood on the walkway. Sometimes it'd be brown and restless in the heat, a great, panting dog. Other days it would be still and shiny as pale-green glass, stinking like the fish stall in Lewisham market. At twilight it would glow pink and gold, touched with tender pools of blue light and smelling yeasty and sweet. At night it flopped and slurped black and angry in the moonlight, a light whiff of sewage.

We loved it. We loved its moods and twists and stenches, we loved searching the silty shore for washed-up junk, or hanging out in the vacant lots, the scrap and boat-yards that flanked its edge. We loved the little houses that lined the nearby cobbled streets, the power stations and the jetties, the boats and muddy swans, the driftwood and the cranes and the mountains of scrap metal reflected in its endless pull and tug. We loved it.

One evening on our way home we stopped at the Quaggy to smoke a cigarette. We hung over the railings, staring down at the putrid green water below us. Next to us on a bench was a pile of empty beer cans. Kyle pointed at a shopping trolley that was half-submerged in the muck and said, 'Bet I can hit that before either of you can.'

We divided the cans between us and started firing them at the trolley. I was first to hit it square on the wheel and Kyle turned to me with one of his rare smiles. 'Not bad,' he said, pursing his lips and nodding admiringly.

'Not bad at all.' Happiness exploded in my guts. I grinned back at him like a moron, far too chuffed to try and look cool.

And then it happened. None of us had seen them coming. Mike, Marco, Lee and this other kid called Dean just appeared out of nowhere. It was like someone had suddenly thrown a black blanket over us. Marco and Lee grabbed hold of me and Denis, and Mike and Dean grabbed Kyle. Within seconds they had him over the railings, dangling him by his ankles so he swung twenty metres above the Quaggy. When I struggled, Marco just held my arms tighter.

'Think you're fucking comedian, don't you?' Mike was shouting down to Kyle. 'Think you're well funny! Not fucking laughing now though, are you? Last person who slagged off my family ended up in hospital, you pikey little cunt.' I was certain they were going to drop Kyle on his head and I didn't know what to do. Every time I struggled, Marco would slap my head and tighten his hold. It seemed to go on for hours.

But suddenly Lee shouted, 'Old Bill!', and I could have cried with relief when I saw the police car pull up next to us. The two coppers stared out at us, bored, their engine growling irritably. Mike and Dean had Kyle pulled back over the railings in a second. They legged it across the road, disappearing down a side-street. The police didn't even bother to get out of the car, just watched Kyle gasping bug-eyed on the pavement for a few moments, then drove on.

The three of us stared at each other, too stunned to speak. Then suddenly Kyle sped off, his skinny little legs powering on double speed. When Denis and I caught him up he wouldn't look at us. 'If I see that cunt again I will kill him,' he said, his voice tight with rage. He stared straight ahead, his face and fists clenched. 'I will fucking kill him. I will get a hammer and beat his head to a fucking pulp. Or I will get a knife and stab him in the face or I will stand on his neck until he can't breathe any more. I fucking would, you know.' He turned to glare at me as if I was going to argue about it. I could think of nothing to say; could only stare at him, mesmerised.

★ ★ ★

A few days later Kyle came and knocked for me and we walked round to Denis's house. I was relieved to see his place was as shit as mine. We rang the doorbell on the peeling yellow door and it played 'Onward Christian

Soldiers'. Immediately a lady no taller than me with a helmet of hair like a Playmobil figure opened the door, like she'd been waiting there ready in case anyone should call. It was Gloria, Denis's mum. Her skin was blue-black and shiny as a beetle. Everything about her was tiny: her hands, her slippers, her eyes. She looked at me suspiciously, her nose wrinkling like a raisin. I couldn't believe she was related to Denis. He was twice the size of her.

'Yes, dear?' Before I could answer she spied Kyle standing behind me. 'Oh, it's you.' She said sullenly, not hiding her disappointment.

'Is Denis in?' I asked.

She stood aside. 'Come on then.' She kissed her teeth quietly as me and Kyle walked past her into the hot brown hall. 'Den!' she screeched up the stairs, her voice surprisingly loud. 'Visitors!'

Gloria nodded at us to follow her into the kitchen where she sat at the table and stared stonily at Kyle. Kyle stared back at her. I looked around the room. It was plastic and shiny and as clean and tidy as ours was messy. Gospel played on the radio. The wall was covered in brightly coloured religious pictures like you used to find at Deptford market for 50p. A plastic Jesus on a plastic cross was pinned on the wall above the sink,

Christ's garish face contorted in cartoon shades of grief.

On the mantelpiece above a gas fire was a framed photo of Denis. It was the one used later by all the newspapers. The famous one, where he's wearing the red and blue sweatshirt and his face is all round and shiny and happy and he looks a bit like that kid from 'Different Strokes'. I reckon the newspaper people deliberately picked a photo where he looked a total flid, for the same reasons they made so much of his church-going and learning difficulties and picked that photo of Kyle looking even more rat-faced and cold-eyed than usual. God knows where they got that one of me. Push, I expect.

I looked at a banner pinned to the wall. It said, 'Repent and ye shall be saved.' Denis's mum followed my gaze.

'What's your name, dear?' she asked, so I told her.

'Have you found Jesus yet, Anita?' she said.

I looked down at my feet. 'Um . . . ' I bit my lip.

'Blessed are the pure in heart, Anita,' said Gloria, sternly. 'For they shall see God. Matthew, five, verse eight.' Her little brown eyes bored into me.

I heard Kyle breathing loudly beside me, and out of the corner of my eye saw his mouth twitch. I looked away, sucking the insides of my cheeks. Luckily, at that moment Denis came bounding in. As usual, his big, dumb face looked made up to see us. You just couldn't ever catch Denis in a bad mood. His mum immediately jumped up and started fiddling with him. She brushed fluff off his T-shirt and pulled his trousers higher. 'You're not going to get yourself all dirty now are you, Denis?' she said, reaching up to cup his podgy cheek in her tiny hand. 'And don't be late. We got to do the flowers in the church tomorrow and you know you promised Reverend Gary that you'd keep up with your reading over the summer.'

I heard a squeak from Kyle and knew that if I met his eyes we'd both start pissing ourselves. Denis shot us a suspicious look. 'Oh Mum, I gotta go. Leave off!'

We piled out into the street. Denis walked in silence for a while, shooting anxious glances to me and Kyle. But we didn't take the piss. We always kept our noses out of each other's business, never talked or asked about each other's lives. When we were together, we had better things to do.

5

**New Cross Hospital. 4 September 1986.
Transcription of interview between Dr C
Barton and Anita Naidu. Police copy.**

*It was really cold. I was so cold in the end
I was shaking and my teeth were rattling. I
tried to keep track of how long I was down
there but it just went on and on forever.
Hours. I had a lighter in my pocket but I just
couldn't get the guts up to work it. I didn't
want to see them. I just couldn't face looking
at them. But in the end I got it out. My
hands were shaking so much that I dropped it
and that's when I found it, the shoe, I mean.
I was feeling about on the floor for the lighter
and I felt, it, this little cold wet thing and I
picked it up and I screamed, I couldn't help
it, I screamed and screamed and I just
couldn't stop screaming once I'd started
because it was a little girl's shoe, a little girl's
red shoe and that was the most horrible thing
of all, that really freaked me out, because I
knew what it meant, I knew whose it was.
I went to the top of the steps then, just threw
myself at the boards, I was banging and*

banging on them, screaming and screaming but they wouldn't budge, not even a little bit and in the end I went back down and curled up because I knew there wasn't any point in screaming anymore. I didn't know you could be that scared.

At the factory today Linda Bennet, the new girl who works in packaging, sliced her finger off with the guillotine. I only realised what was going on when I glanced up and saw the crowd of people huddled around her. Only then did I hear her screams. Somebody had wrapped her severed finger in some tissue and wrapped her wounded hand up too and Linda held her bloody finger in her bloody hand and screamed and screamed and screamed. An endless wailing drone of loss and shock and horror. It made my head hurt. I went back to my sticky labels and thought back to a time when I was a little girl in Leeds.

I must have been about five. Susan Price was my best friend. She was in my class and lived two streets away and we did everything together. On this one, cold, sunny, winter's day my mum drove us to the park in our old white Ford. It had faded red leather seats and rattled. Susan and I were in the back, wrapped in coats and scarves and mittens, beside ourselves with excitement to be going to the swings. It seemed to take forever. We were both screaming and laughing and carrying on, working ourselves into a frenzy of giggles, desperate to escape the hot car and get to the park, to the swings and the slides and to run and run under the sky. My mum was singing along to the radio as she drove us through flashing sunlight.

When the car finally stopped, Susan and I tumbled out and despite my mother calling after us to come back, we ran to the top of a steep, grassy hill on the edge of the park. For only a moment we looked down at the swings and slide and duck pond far away at the bottom, and without a word but at exactly the same time, Susan and I lay down and began to roll down the hill. I was wearing a pink, puffy, nylon jacket with a hood, and as I rolled faster and faster, the hood flipped up to cover my face. Faster and faster I rolled and with every turn the cold, hard grass and mud, then the pink nylon hood, then the shining sky jumped up to meet me. Grass, hood, sky, grass, hood, sky. I remember being hot and sweaty in my coat, I remember my cold nose, the grassy smells, my mother's voice calling and calling my name from the top of the hill, laughter and excitement in my throat. Hood, grass, sky, hood, grass, sky, round and round and over and over wrapped in hot clammy pinkness until I was laughing so hard I could scarcely breathe.

At the bottom Susan and I collided and we lay for a moment side by side just looking up at the shining blue sky streaked with powdery clouds. I remember thinking that it looked as if a giant wearing welly boots had trodden flour into the blueness. Then Susan and I gazed at each other and laughed and laughed and laughed, the warm air bubbling from our mouths into the freezing air. Every inch of me laughed, even my eyelashes were happy.

When my mother finally reached us, out of breath and cross, she gazed at us whooping and spluttering at the sky for a few moments until she shook her head and sighed and smiled and said, 'Oh, you funny little buggers. What am I ever going to do with you?'

That was happiness. *That* was love.

★　★　★

I must have been smiling because suddenly Candice Stamp, who also works in sticky labels, was thrusting her white, doughy face in mine and hissing like a gas leak, 'It's not funny, you bloody weirdo,' and there I was, back in the factory, Linda's howls of pain filling my ears once more.

★ ★ ★

I was twenty yesterday. Look, there on my table is a card from Malcolm. It's there, next to my collection of newspaper cuttings: my file of pre-teen terrorists, adolescent assassins, mini murderers.

Six weeks ago I got home from the shops to find Malcolm standing outside my door. Just standing there staring at his feet. I didn't have a clue what to do. Stupid I suppose but I am so unused to speaking to people I couldn't quite remember how to, for a second. If there had been anyone watching I guess we'd have looked quite comical. Both of us just standing there, frozen, him staring at his feet, me staring at the door, neither of us speaking.

Nothing happened for a bit. Finally he said, 'My name's Malcolm.' He stammered a little over his name. 'Anita,' I said. It came out as a squeak. He asked me if I wanted to go for a walk with him on Saturday morning. I said, 'OK then'. He said he'd meet me outside the flats at ten then. I nodded. We stood there in silence for a second or two then he walked off suddenly, really quickly, down the corridor to his flat. And I was so shocked that I just stood there for a few moments, staring at the bit of air he'd just been standing in. When I got in my flat I sat on my bed in my coat, still holding my plastic bag with my beans and milk in it, my heart going like the clappers until I realised, suddenly, that I had been sitting, there, in the dark, in my coat, holding my shopping for a very long time.

Sometimes I lie on the little bed here and listen to the kids playing in the street below, their taunts and shrieks drifting past my window, their laughter filled with casual cruelty, easy threat. The memories come easily. I can smell the sweet stench of molasses from the animal-feed factory, see the muddy roll of the river, hear Denis talking nonsense, feel the sun on my face. I remember the view from Point Hill, the creek filled with ducks and shopping trolleys and dead branches with twigs like clawing, drowning fingers, how Denis and I hung on Kyle's every word.

Every morning Kyle would knock for me and we'd walk around the corner to pick up Denis. One day they took me to their secret hideout. It wasn't much of a place but I was made up to go there. Along the river past the power station, through the patches of empty wasteland that reeked of those musky white flower-bushes, past the gasworks and scrap-yards then out through the grounds of an old, deserted factory. Kyle and Denis led me to a small redbricked outbuilding that lay crumbling in the dust and the heat. It was empty apart from a couple of broken chairs and a beaten-up metal chest.

Kyle opened it and pulled out a cardboard box containing his cave-finding stash. I looked through it. Library books months out of date on subterranean London, a map of the Thames' banks from Woolwich to Rotherhithe, a plan he'd drawn himself of Greenwich Park, red crosses dotted, apparently randomly (signalling, I found out later, the entrances to the water conduits), a torch, some rope, and a small, rather crappy-looking penknife.

I leafed through one of the books. It fell open on some black and white sketches of the cave Kyle had told me about, the chalk mine under Point Hill. Kyle watched me. 'There are other mines nearby,' he said. 'Sand mines. You can only get to them by breaking into people's back gardens, apparently.' Something about his face told me he'd already tried that. So that's where you go to at night, I thought.

He took the book from me and leafed through it until he found what he was looking for. 'Listen to this,' he said, then started reading, ''A report from the Greenwich

Borough Council in 1914 describes another sand mine in the Greenwich area. It says, 'One can wander about in what seems to be a perfect maze of tunnels for a considerable distance'. The mine described on the previous page is nothing as great as this report suggests so there must either be further workings beyond the roof collapses or another mine as yet unfound.''

Kyle snapped the book shut, a glint of excitement in his eyes and repeated, 'Another mine as yet unfound. But I'm going to find it,' he whispered. 'I'm going to find it if it fucking kills me.'

★   ★   ★

They seemed endless, those long hot days. The summer stretched before us and felt to me to be more real than anything else in my life before had been, or since, come to think of it. It was like every bit of me was concentrated into those weeks, that they eclipsed everything, both my past and my future. That summer was like a flaming meteor tearing through blackness, through nothingness. And I sensed that I would always feel that way about it, for the rest of my life.

When we weren't looking for caves we'd go

to the park and look for the entrances to the conduits. Other days we'd get the bus to Woolwich to watch the boats but mainly we'd hang around the river's edge in Greenwich, climbing the fences into the old boat-yards or breaking into the scrap heaps looking for stuff to nick. Sometimes Denis would bring food from home and we'd make little fires to cook it on. It always tasted like shit but it made us feel intrepid, like we could live out there forever if necessary, on our wits and burnt bits of bacon.

★　★　★

Neither Kyle nor I were big talkers, and a lot of the time we'd just listen to Denis banging on, his endless stories and tangents on anything from cavemen to his favourite kind of cake a running soundtrack to whatever we were doing that day. When Kyle did speak I'd hold onto his every word, turning them over in my mind like marbles when I was alone. And as I've said, none of us ever really mentioned our families, though of course I was still desperately curious about Kyle's. Which is why I remember so clearly, and was so surprised, by something he said one day.

We were sitting by the river as usual and I was half listening to Denis going on about crocodiles in Africa. I only really started paying attention when I heard him say, 'That's where my dad is.' I looked at him, an eyebrow raised, and he said, 'It's true! No lies! My dad's a missionary in Africa.'

I probably said something along the lines of 'Yeh, right,' or 'Bollocks' because I remember Denis going, 'No lies! He *is* in Africa and it's true because my mum told me.'

It seemed very important to him that we believed him, so he kept going on about it, elaborating more and more, and I kept making the same 'Bollocks' face all the way through, just to wind him up.

'He goes all over the world, he does,' Denis was saying, 'he's spreading the word of our Lord.' He said it so solemnly I sniggered, and Denis blurted in desperation, 'In fact, he probably isn't even in Africa any more, he's probably gone to America by now, he's probably in Disney Land with . . .'

I started laughing, 'With who?' I asked.

'Edward Woodward,' he said lamely, then bit his lip while I pissed myself.

That's when Kyle said, not looking at us, almost to himself, 'My dad's in America'.

'Really?' I said, a bit too eagerly.

'He moved there when him and Mum split up,' he said, then he turned his slate-grey eyes on me. 'He wanted to take me and my sister with him but . . . ' he stopped then, and looked off into the distance. I nodded, silently urging him to go on, 'But they wouldn't have it. Granddad and Mum. They wouldn't have it. So we moved down here instead. And Dad went to America.'

He shrugged, looked away, and then continued gazing out to the river. I was so stunned that he had brought up Katie that I didn't know what to say. I had been so curious about his sister's disappearance, so desperate to ask him about it and yet so certain that it was off-limits, that I couldn't quite believe he'd mentioned her like that. I tried to work up the courage to ask him about her, but I knew it was hopeless the moment he shifted his big, cold eyes back to me, blinked his dismissal, then got up and walked to the edge of the river to throw stones into the water.

★ ★ ★

A couple of days later on our way back towards Greenwich we stopped to watch a tramp sitting on a bench near the jetty. Denis was endlessly fascinated by tramps for some reason. This one kept swigging from a bottle and talking to himself. Now and then he'd start shouting and waving his arms around, spraying wine onto passing tourists. As I watched, a picture of my dad popped into my head. I imagined him dressed in piss-stained clothes with broken teeth and a dirty, big beard. I found myself wondering how much of a jump it might be, from sitting day in, day out in front of the TV with a dole cheque's worth of lager, to raving through the streets shouting at lampposts. I shuddered and turned to Kyle but the sight of him made me catch my breath.

I was used to Kyle by then; his mood swings, the way he would sink without trace sometimes like a bottle filled with dirty river water. He'd be stood there beside you, but you knew he wasn't really. It made you feel a bit anxious when it happened, a bit panicky. Like that feeling you get when you walk into a room and you think you can smell gas but you're not really sure. Usually Denis and I just waited these moods out, talked between ourselves until he came back to us. But as I watched him gaze at the tramp I felt there was something wrong, something particularly strange about his stillness and his silence. 'Kyle?' I said, but he didn't seem to hear. He had his big coat on that day and I remember thinking that he looked little, suddenly — like a much smaller boy.

I touched his arm and he turned to face

me. I remember I actually backed away so quickly I stepped on Denis's foot and he yelped. He looked like someone else, as if someone who hated me had crept into his head and was now looking out at me with those eyes of Kyle's. I felt as stunned as if he'd reached out and gripped me by the throat. He had been fine five minutes before that and the change in him was sudden and violent and it freaked the fuck out of me. And yet I understood somehow too that this stranger had always been lurking, treading water there beneath the surface.

'Kyle,' I said. 'What's wrong?'

And then suddenly he just went. Just walked off like he was in a massive rush to be somewhere else. Denis and I stood for a moment watching his back as he weaved his way through the tourists, then we hurried after him.

It was eight o'clock; usually by that time we'd have started thinking about going home, so I was surprised when he kept on towards Deptford. As we walked, the sky turned slowly from blue to pink to orange, tendrils of red spilling across the sky like broken blood vessels. Following the river we passed a couple of council estates, their forecourts full of kids and smashed-up cars, saris and tracksuits hanging over balconies, music

81

blaring over the Thames from tiny windows.

We stopped by a row of tatty caravans that overlooked a large bit of beach. Some houseboats were docked just beyond it. We followed Kyle over the railings and crunched our way across the muddy pebbles. The darkening sky glowed pink around us, dense with the whiff of the river. In the far corner, tethered to a wooden stake, sat a small rowing boat. We got in and sat side by side on one of the benches, looking across to the Isle of Dogs. This was not tourist territory; no one would even notice we were down there unless they leaned right over the railings to look.

'It must belong to the gypsies,' I said, nodding my head towards the houseboats and caravans. I could smell food cooking, could hear the soft rumble of voices and laughter from the nearest boat. I remember thinking how cosy and warm it sounded, and wished that I belonged there too.

'Come on,' said Kyle.

'Where are we going?' asked Denis. I could tell he was getting worried about his tea. Kyle smiled slightly, an empty smile that set my teeth on edge. 'We're going on a little boat trip.'

The three of us got up and stepped out of the boat. I hoped that he was joking, but then he started untying the rope. 'We don't even have oars,' I said. I looked out towards the river. It seemed very wide suddenly. The twin dome of the foot tunnel on the other side looked far away, the reflections of the lamps dotting the distant bank trailed orange streaks across the darkening water.

'Yes we do,' said Kyle. He hopped over to the other side of the boat and pulled two out from where they'd been hidden. He was full of energy and purpose suddenly, and when he'd finished untying the rope he looked at me and Denis impatiently. 'Well, help me push, then!'

Denis looked at the boat doubtfully, his fingers in his mouth. 'Kyle,' he said, 'I can't swim.'

'Well, you won't need to swim, will you? We've got a fucking boat.'

The edge to Kyle's voice made my heart sink. Reluctantly Denis joined him and together they started pushing. I stayed where I was. 'I really don't think this is a good idea. Seriously, man.'

Kyle stopped pushing. He walked towards me, his eyes boring into mine. I took a step back. He spoke softly, his nasal, London accent thin in the muggy evening air. 'Either help us push, or fuck off home.' He stood there for a moment, staring, then walked back to the boat. I helped them push.

When the boat was finally bobbing about on the water, we got in, Denis and I on one side, Kyle facing us. Kyle used one of the oars to lever us away from the beach and suddenly we were floating, our little boat rocking gently on the water. Kyle paddled us out and in no time at all we were metres away from the edge. The water that had looked so calm from the shore started bobbing more aggressively around us, carrying the boat further out into the middle of the river. We floated past a houseboat, two scruffy kids waving at us from the deck.

Denis gripped the sides and tried to look like he was having fun. I just stared back at the shore, wondering how we were ever going to get back there. The sun was red and low in the sky. The houses and flats and pubs on the river's edge had faded into grey and lights had started to appear in windows. As I watched, two men from one of the caravans appeared and started shouting something at us but I couldn't hear what they said.

We were being carried into the middle of the river, the boat rocking ever more quickly towards Rotherhithe. Kyle tossed the oars into the middle of the boat, sat back and lit a fag butt he'd had in his pocket. I didn't like being so close to the water. Push had told me once that it was full of the dead bodies of suicides and drunks. I knew that he was full of shit but still it made me jumpy. I scanned the murky river for corpses then looked back at Kyle who was gazing blankly ahead, the red-hued water and its secrets reflected in his eyes.

I tried to keep my voice steady. 'Kyle,' I said, 'I think maybe we should . . . ' but it was pointless. He was utterly unreachable. He just sat there, puffing away on his fag and staring down at a little puddle in the bottom of the boat, the same, thin non-smile on his face. I don't think he could even hear me. Waves started lapping more aggressively at our boat suddenly, and I looked up to see the last commuter ferry of the day heading towards us. We began to rock back and forth, water spilling over the sides onto our feet. I decided to take matters into my own hands.

'Denis,' I said, trying to keep the panic out of my voice. 'Pass me the oars.' Denis reached down and Kyle put his foot on his wrist. 'Leave it.'

'Kyle, for fuck's sake!'

I was too scared now to care about him being angry. But he just kept looking down at the puddle, and I realised then that he didn't care. He really didn't give a flying fuck if we all drowned. The realisation hit me like icy liquid shooting up my spine. A slow panic rose in my chest. Suddenly a long wailing horn blasted; the ferry was nearly upon us and our little boat started rocking more wildly, the edges dipping further each time into the water. Denis started crying.

I made a grab for the oars and Kyle kicked my hand. 'Leave it you fucking Paki cunt.' It was a stranger's voice.

He'd kicked my hand really hard, and I gazed from it, to his face, in disbelief. 'What did you call me?' I asked stupidly. But I had no time to dwell on it. In a sudden panic Denis had stood up and started flailing for the oars. What happened next isn't clear, even to me. Did Kyle actually, purposely, kick him into the river or did he just kick him away from the oars? Whatever — it had the same effect. Denis lost his balance and fell backwards into the Thames.

It's funny the things you notice in moments of panic. I remember, as I reached out to grab Denis's flailing arms as he sank and splashed and resurfaced, the faces of the passengers of the commuter ferry as they hung over the railings to watch us. I saw a little blonde girl laughing as if delighted at the fat kid splashing and screaming in the water below her. I turned to Kyle and said desperately, 'Help me, Kyle. Help me hold onto him.' And in that split second, as if blinking awake from a coma, Kyle's eyes cleared and he helped me hold onto Denis's arms.

Suddenly we heard an engine roaring behind us, a loudspeaker, a cheer from the ferry. The little blue and black police boat reached us in no time.

★   ★   ★

The three of us didn't speak in the police car as it drove us back from Rotherhithe, Denis wet and shivering between me and Kyle on the back seat. The two policemen however had plenty to say and didn't hold back the entire journey. It turned out we were stupid little bastards and they had far better things to do with their time than fish thieving shitheads out of the Thames.

We stopped at Denis's first. The tall, skinny, blond copper rocked on his heels as the doorbell played its hymn. I could tell from his back that Denis was shitting it. At last Gloria opened the door, her little eyes narrowing even smaller as she stared suspiciously out at the man in uniform with her son. The policeman talked, Gloria threw her hands to the sky and Denis hung his head. Eventually she said something to the copper, wagged her finger in his face, pulled Denis into the house and slammed the door, but not before she shot a low, mean look into the backseat of the car where me and Kyle sat. 'Fucking nutter,' muttered the policeman as he got in again beside his mate. We drove on.

Next stop was Kyle's. The policemen told me to stay where I was and they both got out and walked him to his front door. When Patrick answered their knock I remember thinking the first look on his face was strange. It was fleeting, the fear that flashed into his eyes, but it was definitely there. Just for that split second he looked straight at Kyle and he looked terrified. Within a moment though, it was replaced by worried concern as he listened to what the coppers had to say. After a while he started talking and although I couldn't hear what he said there was a grace and intelligence about the old man, a calmness that I could see and feel even from where I sat in the car. I somehow knew, from the way they stood and listened and nodded, that the coppers were impressed by him; respected him in a way they hadn't respected Gloria and wouldn't respect my dad. Finally Patrick must have cracked a joke because the two policemen suddenly lost their air of irritated self-righteousness and started laughing, raised their hats, then turned back to the car, and me.

It took ages for someone to open our front door. The policemen stood stony-faced before our unimposing pebble-dash and the three of us waited in silence. They looked disapprovingly at a pile of beer cans by our bin. I wanted to tell them it wasn't my fault that a bomb had fallen long ago and destroyed the proper houses that should have still stood there. It wasn't my fault they'd put this row of council homes there instead. It wasn't my fault Kyle was such a fucking lunatic, either. But I just kept my mouth shut and wished that someone would hurry up and come.

When Push saw me with the two policemen he went boggle-eyed with excitement. 'Daaaaaaaaaad!' he yelled over his shoulder, then turned back to gape at me. After a few minutes my dad appeared, dazed and baffled in his cardigan. The coppers towered over him and he shrank back, blinking.

'Mr Naidu?' said the first copper. 'Is this your daughter?'

Dad looked at me, doubtfully. 'Yes?'

'We found her in the Thames, Mr Naidu. She and her friends had stolen a boat.'

Push let out a whistle and looked at me agog. 'A boat?' he spluttered. 'You stole a fucking boat?' He waved his right hand, making a clicking sound like he'd seen the black kids at school do. 'Oh, man!'

The blond copper looked at my dad and brother with distaste. He hadn't had the chance to be very impressive on Patrick's doorstep, and I could tell he was going to make up for it on mine. 'It was potentially a very dangerous situation, Mr Naidu,' he began, drawing himself up to his full height and squaring his puny shoulders. He consulted his notebook and spoke like he was in the dock of the Old Bailey. 'The incident involved not just the theft of private property, Mr Naidu, but also risked the lives of a number of the general public.'

And so on and so on. The policeman just kept talking and talking at Dad, probably trying to get some sort of reaction from him. I could have told them they'd be there all night, but I sensed it was probably better if I kept my mouth shut. Finally Janice appeared and shoved her way, tits first, in front of Dad. She beamed at the blond one, grabbed my shoulder and pulled me firmly inside behind her. As I went up the stairs I heard her say, 'She's usually such a good girl, Officer, but there's been a recent death in the family and I'm afraid . . . ' I closed my bedroom door and lay down.

After ten minutes my dad came. I don't

think I'd ever seen him in my room before. He sat down on Bela's bed and looked around in amazement, his gaze finally resting on a pair of tights wrapped around an empty bottle of vodka. Neither of us spoke. I pulled at some loose wallpaper and watched him. Eventually he tried a smile and said, 'Didn't take you for the nautical type, Ani.'

I hated it when he called me that. I shrugged. 'Things just got out of hand.'

My father looked at me then and sighed. 'Do you . . . ' he stopped

'What?' I said, more aggressively than I'd meant.

My dad flinched. 'I'm sorry, Nita.' He said finally. He shook his head and tried again. 'I'm sorry I haven't been . . . '

Oh God. Not this. The last thing I needed was this. I interrupted him. 'Look, Dad, it's all right. Really. Just don't worry about it.' I turned away and started fiddling with the telly.

He sat there for a few minutes longer, but eventually gave up and opened the door. As he left he turned and said, 'OK. But if you . . . ' he gazed at me, then shuffled back out of the room. Twenty seconds later I heard the *Bullseye* theme tune blaring from the lounge.

I lay on my bed and thought about when it

was that my dad and I had stopped being able to bear being in the same room together. It was like an icy wind had just drifted in sometime after Mum had died; a coldness that had circled around and around looking for somewhere comfortable to rest, until without warning it had plotted down between the two of us. A stubborn, watchful and uneasy ghost.

But maybe it had always been that way. It was odd, because in a lot of ways we were the same, me and Dad. And yet we took no comfort in each other; we much preferred the company of Mum and Push and the twins, felt more at ease with happy, outgoing people, who didn't shrink from the world like we did. And maybe we felt Mum's death more than the others, perhaps we suffered more than them. But it was almost as if recognising it in each other only made things worse. So we avoided one another, pretended not to notice how badly her death had affected us.

Or maybe he just never forgave me for all the time my mother had focused on me before she died, the attention that she used to give me. He never really understood the need for that.

I thought about the things that had started happening to me way back in my past that had made it necessary to close myself off, keep myself in check and not let anyone guess at the secrets that I kept. The secrets only Mum knew about. I felt exhausted suddenly with the effort of it all, with the loneliness of it.

I must have fallen asleep, because the next thing I knew it was pitch-black and my heart was banging in my chest, my pillow wet with sweat. I'd dreamt that I was running down a very long, very narrow tunnel. Kyle was chasing me and no matter how fast I ran I knew he was catching up. Ahead of me behind every bend, I could hear my mother calling, 'Keep running, Anita, I'm here.' But every time I thought she'd be just around the next corner the tunnel would twist and turn away from me and there would be only blackness ahead.

★   ★   ★

Of course we weren't going to get away with stealing a boat and nearly crashing it into a ferry without a bollocking. But I realise now that Patrick must have come to some sort of arrangement with the police. They knew him down the local nick, and knowing Patrick he must have charmed them into letting us off with a warning. I knew none of this at the time though and when Patrick and Kyle collected me two days later on their way to Brockley Police Station, I was bricking it.

We walked to Denis's house first, Kyle and I silent, Patrick humming to himself. When Denis answered the door he shot one agonised look at the three of us then stood aside to let Patrick pass before joining me and Kyle on the street.

We stood on the pavement and waited for Patrick to come back out. 'Do you think they're going to put us in prison?' asked Denis. He looked like he was going to cry.

Kyle looked bored. ''Course not, dickhead,' he said. 'They don't put kids in prison.'

'My mum says we're all going to hell,' said Denis. 'For stealing.'

Kyle shot him a contemptuous look, but said nothing. Finally, Patrick appeared. I saw Gloria behind him, but she didn't say a word.

At the police station we walked into the reception to find two policemen behind the desk. They didn't notice us come in. The first one was bald and chubby and was busy mopping up some spilt coffee. 'Fuck's sake, Alan,' he was saying. 'You're such a clumsy bastard.'

The second policeman smirked. 'Calm down, Jim, it's only a bit of coffee. Let's not turn a rape into murder.' They both roared with laughter.

Patrick cleared his throat then smiled easily as the two men blushed and straightened. 'PC Baxter?' asked Patrick. He strode over, offering his hand. 'We spoke on the phone. I'm Patrick Morgan.'

'Ah yes, of course, Mr Morgan.' The bald chubby one led the three of us into a little room and left us there. As we passed out of the reception I heard the one called Alan clear his throat and say, 'Hope you don't mind my saying, sir, but I remember you from the, er, business last year. Sure it must still be very difficult for you . . . '

But Patrick silenced him with a stiff, 'Quite.'

We were left in that room for forty minutes. The three of us sat in silence, watching the minute hand of the clock loudly click away each sixty seconds. After quarter of an hour Denis started snuffling and gulping next to me. 'Look, don't worry,' I said with more confidence than I felt. 'They're just going to give us a bollocking, that's all.'

Denis wiped his snotty nose with his sleeve. 'What if they send us to prison, though?' he asked.

Kyle kicked the table leg in irritation. 'Stop being such a gaylord, Denis,' he said. 'We stole a fucking boat, we didn't kill anyone.'

Finally the two coppers came in, shouted at

us for ten minutes about wasting police time, stealing, and how if we did anything — anything — at all again, we'd be deeply fucking sorry. Denis and I looked at our shoes the entire time. I heard Denis start sniffing again.

By the end of that summer, of course, I was to become quite used to dealing with policemen. But back then it was my first time inside a station even, and I was scared.

Suddenly the bald copper stopped. 'You're a cocky little fucker, aren't you, lad?'

I followed his gaze to Kyle who was staring insolently back at the policeman. Finally Kyle just shrugged, then looked away. At last they let us go.

Outside I didn't say anything to the other two. I was sick to death of Kyle suddenly; sick to death of the duck-murdering, boat-stealing sight of him, sick to my stomach with trying to work out his secrets and his silences. So I left them standing there without saying goodbye, telling myself that Kyle could swivel — I was fucked if I was going to see him again.

6

After the boat episode, I stayed away from Kyle for a couple of days. It felt like weeks. I can see you don't understand, Doctor Barton. Why would I miss someone who behaved the way he did? What could I like about someone like that? Let me try to explain. I had never met anyone like him before. He was so certain of himself, so utterly unconcerned by what others thought of him. He had a confidence and a disregard for the 'proper' way of doing things that I found infinitely impressive. And if Kyle showed an interest in something I said, it meant that I was interesting. Simple as that. If he turned away from me, the sun went in.

Whatever we did, wherever we went, it was always his idea. It was him who knew about the mines under Greenwich, his idea to hunt for a cave where we would, perhaps, live one day, the three of us in our own little underground world. And we were kids, you know? Just kids who don't cast aside friendships for random acts of madness. When you're a kid you tend to see the best in your mates. Because at least they're not as mad as your fucking parents.

So, a couple of days without seeing them and I was missing Kyle and Denis like crazy. Denis and I never went and knocked for Kyle; it was an unspoken rule of ours, so I had to wait to see if he turned up. Of course he didn't. Finally Dad gave me a quid out of his dole money and asked me to go into Lewisham to buy a birthday present for Auntie Jam. Ordinarily I would have resented doing anything for the bitch, but it gave me an excuse to get out of the house and walk past Denis's, to see if he wanted to come with me.

Nobody answered when I knocked so I walked to the Army & Navy store by myself. The shop was empty. Sadé played over the loudspeakers to no one and the place smelt the way failing department stores usually do; that bright, plasticy smell masking something a bit musty and hopeless. Like expensive perfume on a pissy old-age pensioner.

Under the strip-lighting and through the aisles of toiletries I trailed, past bath cubes and face flannels and soaps on dusty shelves. Eventually I stuffed a few boxes of talc up my T-shirt and left by the nearest exit. It had been as easy as it had always been, in those long empty school-less days in Leeds after

Mum died. I was glad to see I hadn't lost my touch.

When I got to Myre Street, the pound still in my pocket, I looked across to No. 33. Kyle's house always looked desolate, but I knew that didn't necessarily mean no one was in. The curtains were drawn as usual, the glass perpetually black in the sunshine of those days. When I let myself into our house it was empty. No music playing upstairs, no Dad watching telly, no Janice laughing in the kitchen. The emptiness was so unusual I just stood in the hall, the talc boxes digging into my skin, and listened to it for a while. Everything was perfectly still and I remember thinking how nice it was. As I listened to the empty house I began, as you do, picking out the tiny slivers of sound that constitute its silence. The ticking of the fridge, a radio playing in somebody's garden, the barking of next-door's dog. And somewhere, the soft, low murmur of a woman crying.

What was that? Suddenly it was the only sound I could hear. An almost imperceptible 'huh-huh-huh' noise, the whereabouts of which I couldn't identify. I walked towards the foot of the stairs, my movements drowning it out momentarily. But there it was again. I walked upstairs and it got louder. Thinking it was one of my sisters I opened the door to our bedroom. It was empty and I realised then the noise was coming from my dad's room. The door was ajar and I pushed it open.

It took a few moments to work out what was happening. Janice seemed to be kneeling, naked, on my dad's bed. I stood in the doorway totally bewildered by the sight of her vast, sweaty flesh as it wobbled and heaved spam-like in the midday heat, her breasts swinging almost to her navel, tufts of orange glistening from her pits and crotch. In a sort of stupid horror I watched her bounce and gyrate her massive hips, an angry red groove running across them where her knickers had once been, and wondered what strange madness it was that had led her to this. I thought she was in some sort of terrible trance. Her eyes were closed and she was still making the moaning noise I'd heard from downstairs. I wondered how the hell I was going to wake her.

Stupid, wasn't I? Because then of course I saw something brown and skinny wriggling between her thighs. I hadn't noticed him before because he'd been half-covered by Janice and the duvet, but it was my dad under there, naked and silent under our neighbour's massive weight. I couldn't see his face but I recognised him by the hand he raised suddenly, to bat half-heartedly at one of Janice's pinkywhite udders. I knew it was my dad by the wedding ring he still wore then.

I backed out of the door and down the stairs and out of the house, into the burning midday heat. And though I don't remember making the decision to go and knock on Kyle's door, though I only recall my heart thumping and a sort of bleak shame and rage, there I was suddenly, watching my hand reach up and bang the huge brass knocker. Too late I realised the mistake I'd made and could only stare anxiously up at the three storeys of yellow brick, the dark unfriendly windows and high pointing roof, knowing how angry Kyle would be to see me on his step and that it was too late to run away. Then the door opened and there stood Patrick, blinking into the sun.

'Anita!' he said, as if delighted, and I'm afraid I felt flattered to hear him speak my name. He had that sort of effect on you, Kyle's granddad. And as if it was the most natural thing in the world, as if I dropped round like that every day, he stood aside, smiling, and ushered me in. I forgot all about Janice and my dad then. I had wondered so often about the inside of Kyle's house that I could only gaze around me in silence, like a kid on a school trip to a museum, overawed by its differentness to anywhere I'd ever been before.

The hallway was dark after the intense brightness of the street. It was quiet and still with black and white diamond tiles on the floor, a wide uncarpeted staircase and a dank and heavy feel to the air as if it hadn't been disturbed for years. I'd never been in a house like that before. If I'm honest, I'd never been in a house that wasn't modern and small and crap like ours and Denis's was.

Patrick showed me into their front room and looked at me curiously when I gasped. It was huge. Red velvet curtains hung from the bay windows and behind them the sun burned, bathing the room in a soft, orange glow. Through the gaps in the curtains the light lasered in great dustinfested shafts. It was hot and still and thrilling to me. The place was full of antique furniture, the walls covered in gold and green wallpaper. An immense Persian rug covered the floorboards and in front of an enormous marble fireplace stood a china vase full of peacock feathers.

I stood, gazing around the room until I finally noticed that in front of the window was a large oak table on which lay a small-scale model of a battle scene. Noticing me staring, Patrick smiled and ushered me over to it. Across the fuzzy green hills and valleys were perched hundreds of tiny, exquisitely painted lead figures.

'The Borodino battlefield,' explained Patrick. I must have looked blank because then he went on, 'From the Napoleonic war. The soldiers in red are the Russians, the blue ones are the French.'

I stared at it for a long time. Some of the little soldiers sat atop perfectly rendered horses in various states of charge or collapse, and there were cannons and ammunition carts, bloodstained corpses and discarded bayonets all carefully arranged in perpetual gory massacre. Each soldier's face was unique in its expression of aggression, fear, or death. On the highest hill the lone, squat figure of Napoleon stood, surveying the carnage below.

'Beautiful craftsmanship,' said Patrick plucking a tiny figure skewered on a bayonet. 'Look at the detail!' He turned the soldier around and showed me where the point of the sword went right through his back, the wound spewing faded orangey-red guts like raw mince.

'Smashing,' I said, which seemed to please Patrick greatly, and he beamed at me as if I were the most charming and eloquent person he had ever met. I continued gazing around the room. At first glance it was elegant, grand, expensive, but when you looked more closely you realised that everything was a bit fucked. Every surface was covered in crap: spilt coffee, empty cups, stacks of books, broken ornaments, dust. I looked up at the beautiful silk light shade and saw that it was ripped, noticed that the rug and curtains were threadbare and stained, that the chaiselongue sagged where the springs had broken.

Eventually I turned back to Patrick. I know you'll think this stupid, but I don't care, I'll say it anyway. I turned to look at Kyle's granddad, standing there in that beautiful chaotic room and I think I started to love him right at that moment. Of course I don't mean I fancied him, he was past sixty and I was thirteen. It was different from that. I felt an overwhelming jealousy suddenly that he was Kyle's and not mine.

He was impressive for his age, tall and handsome in his smart old-man's clothes and touched I thought with a kind of magic and glamour — charisma I suppose you'd call it. But it was his kindness I loved. I'd only just met him but I sensed that he was the kindest man I'd ever seen. Unusually for me, I felt instantly and entirely at ease with him.

We started talking. He asked me questions about myself, about school and Leeds and my family. I talked more in those twenty minutes than I probably had to any other adult in my entire life apart from Mum. Eventually I wandered over to a framed picture and picked it up. It was of a woman with curly hair, her arms around Kyle and a little blonde girl. Of course I knew immediately who it was and I froze, unsure of what to say.

Patrick came over to where I stood and gently took the picture from me. 'That's Elizabeth,' he said. 'My daughter. And young Kyle, of course.' His finger stroked the little blonde-haired girl. 'And this is little Katie.' As he said the last word his voice was heavy and broken and all fucked-up and even though I didn't know him at all I wanted to say something, anything to make it better. But there was nothing I could think of to say.

Outside in the street someone was banging something with a hammer and each *thwack* bounced loudly off the hot afternoon air. Patrick and I listened to it for a while, and when it stopped suddenly, that final thwack seemed to lengthen and the room and me and Patrick were held within the sound for a while. Isn't it funny how a moment can expand then hold its breath and just sit still like that, suspended, teetering, and then it passes? Have you noticed that, Doctor Barton?

'You and Kyle are great pals, aren't you?' Patrick asked suddenly. I must have looked doubtful but he carried on anyway, in his soft, slightly Scottish accent that made me want to curl up and have a kip on his lap. I can hear that voice still. It mingles with my nightmares.

'I hope,' he trailed off, looking for the right words. 'I think Kyle has been very unhappy.' He looked at me as if I was going to contradict him, but I said nothing. 'I don't think Kyle ever got over it. What happened.'

I held my breath then said, in a whisper, 'What did happen? What happened to Katie, Patrick?'

Patrick stared at me for so long that I thought that I had blown it, that I'd said the wrong thing and that he'd ask me to leave, and the pain of it, of being made to leave that house and go home was almost too much for me to bear. But then he whispered simply, 'I don't know, my dear. I really don't know.'

In the quiet that followed I was dimly aware of floorboards creaking above us, as if someone was pacing upstairs, and also of the sound of faint opera music, a woman wailing something tragic and foreign that wafted down from some far away room, but mainly I was caught up in that silence that fell between us, deeper and darker than any cave. Patrick kept staring down at the photograph and I remember desperately wanting to take one of his big old hands and hold it.

Then, 'What the fuck are you doing?'

I don't know how long Kyle had been standing in the doorway and his voice made me and Patrick jump. He was staring, horrified, as if he'd caught me stealing or something. I could only look back at him dumbly, taking in the awful changes in him since I had last seen him. He looked like shit: wasted, fucked, his eyes sunken into his pale flesh, his greasy hair sticking flat to his skull, his bony wrists translucent, snappable.

It struck me how strange it was that someone could look so physically fragile but could still be so powerful. I suppose people call it presence, or force of personality, but I have never met anyone since who has that ability to alter a room and how you feel in it without saying anything at all. He stood there, a scrawny ghost in the doorway, then he stormed towards us and snatched the photo from Patrick. His granddad reached out and touched his shoulder and Kyle flinched, but that wasn't unusual. Kyle always hated to be touched.

Patrick said nothing for a few moments as he stared gravely at him, and then, 'Where's your mother, Kyle?'

It was a perfectly normal question to ask but Kyle looked uncertain suddenly, the mutiny left his eyes to be replaced with confusion. Almost fearfully he looked over his shoulder. Suddenly in the silence the floorboards resumed their creaking above us, while the three of us listened.

Then, suddenly, Kyle shoved the picture of his family into my hands and strode out of the room and out of the house, slamming the front door behind him. I was stunned. I looked at Patrick, embarrassed suddenly to be there alone with him in that house where Kyle, my friend, wasn't. Confused, I put the picture down and made to follow him but Patrick put his hand out, restraining me.

'Don't go after him, my dear,' he said. 'I wouldn't follow him when he's in that mood.' He smiled ruefully. 'Best to leave him to it.' He put his hands in his pockets and leant against the table, looking at me conspiratorially. 'For that way madness lies.' He winked.

I stared back blankly.

'*King Lear*,' he said, by way of explanation. 'Do you read much Shakespeare, Anita?' As if it was quite likely that I did.

'No,' I muttered and desperately tried to think of something intelligent to say. 'We're doing *To Kill A Mockingbird* at school, though.' I didn't mention that it still lay unread at the bottom of my Co-op bag.

'Ah, I see.' Patrick smiled his sweet, sad smile, and despite not knowing what to say, and knowing that I should leave, and feeling strangely disloyal to Kyle, I smiled back. Patrick went to root through a stack of records in the corner and, pulling one from its sleeve, put it on the old-fashioned record player that sat on one of the dusty antique tables. After the hissing and scratching of the grooves, an old Sinatra track came on.

Somewhere beyond the sea,
Somewhere waiting for me,
My lover stands on golden sands
And watches the ships that go sailing.

I had always liked that song, my mum and dad used to play it sometimes back in Leeds. I liked the way it was happy and sad at the same time. I should have felt embarrassed just standing there in silence while we listened, and ordinarily I would have done, but instead I just thought how graceful and handsome Patrick looked, like an old film star stood there, his thick white hair caught in one of the shafts of light as it spilled through the gaps in the curtains.

Happy we'll be beyond the sea,
And never again, I'll go sailing.

When the song came to an end Patrick smiled

and there was something in his manner that let me know it was time I was leaving. He came with me to the door and suddenly said, 'It's Kyle's birthday on Saturday. He'll be fourteen.'

I felt shocked. Kyle didn't seem to be the sort of person to have birthdays or even to have a definite, tangible age. I'd always thought of him as ageless, somehow, neither a kid nor an adult, just Kyle.

'We must do something special,' Patrick continued, and I tried in vain to imagine Kyle wearing a party hat. Just then, as we stood in the big gloomy hallway, a little girl's voice called down from upstairs and I felt such a quick sharp chill it made my scalp shrivel.

'Daddy?' The voice was querulous, tearful. I stared, horrified, at Patrick.

'Where are you, Daddy?' the voice said again. Then, 'Kyle? Are you there?'

Patrick turned and called back up the stairs, 'I'm coming, Lizzy. Daddy's coming.'

Then I understood. The voice belonged not to a little girl, but to Kyle's mother. She sounded like a child and Patrick certainly spoke to her like she was a child but she wasn't — it was Elizabeth, Kyle and Katie's mum. Everything felt very strange in that hallway suddenly: queasy and off-kilter. I muttered a quick goodbye to Patrick, and left.

★ ★ ★

That night was endless. I'd positioned my bed so my pillow was at the window end and I could look out onto the street. I had bad dreams from which I'd wake, sweating and anxious in the darkness. At about five, I woke again to see the sky had turned violet and as I lay there, staring at the street, I caught a sudden movement outside No. 33. It was Kyle, returning from wherever he'd run off to the afternoon before. I lifted the net higher to watch him. As he let himself into the house he turned suddenly and seemed to look directly at me. Could he see me? I let the net fall and lay staring up at the ceiling, my heart thudding as my sisters slept.

7

New Cross Hospital. 4 September 1986. Transcription of interview between Dr C Barton and Anita Naidu. Police copy.

That little shoe . . . I held it for so many hours . . . couldn't let it go. And then, well in my head it kind of became the most important thing, more important than any-thing else. I held onto it like it could save me, as if it was the only way out, like if I dropped it that would be it. That would be . . . it. Silly, really. Fucking stupid. It was only a shoe.

Damien, Carrie, Mary Bell, that girl from *The Exorcist*, Jon Venables and Robert Thompson, Kyle Kite, Rosemary's frigging baby. All evil little fuckers aren't they? A rotten pick 'n' mix of pint-sized psychos, a fun-bag of stunted freaks: cut out and keep 'em, buy two and get one free.

It's nearly 1994 and the James Bulger Show rages on. The why-why-why of it, the how-how-how of it, the hang-'em-high, string-'em-up, eye-for-an-eye of it. 'A nation

112

grieves' my arse. A nation fucking panics. I watch the news reports of those mobs outside the court and see the hatred in their faces and in the eyes of the girls in my factory ('throw away the key'), the panic in the headlines and the venom on the talk shows. An aimless fucking raging against what? Does anybody even know? Look in your own backyards I want to tell them. Look at your own fucking kids. But their anger is nothing to the loathing, the absolute fury I've felt every single bastard minute of the past seven years since that end-of-summer day, that end-of-everything day when I was thirteen.

★ ★ ★

Push comes sometimes. I've told him not to and sometimes I don't answer the door but still he comes, filling my bedsit with his expensive aftershave and his gold jewellery and his cashmere coat. Sometimes he turns up outside the factory in his BMW ('That your fella, Anita? Bit of all right'). He takes me out to lunch and he talks about his Docklands flat and his girlfriends and his holidays but never where the money actually comes from and I don't ask. He talks and talks, always staring at me, while the waitresses stare at him and I stare at the

113

table. He worries, he says. I don't mind him coming but I don't really like my routine interrupted very much. I like to do things a certain way. I measure out my days carefully, precisely.

★　★　★

After it happened my dad and Janice moved back to Leeds (how I'd have loved to have seen Auntie Jam's face when she copped a load of that). My sisters tried to keep in touch but in the end, when I never replied to their letters or phoned them back, they gave up. They've got their own kids now. I didn't mean to cut them off completely, I just couldn't stand the way they looked at me.

It's the blood, I think. It's the blood nobody can get over. That image the world has of me running through the streets of Greenwich one Saturday lunchtime at the end of summer, my white T-shirt drenched in blood. Blood in my hair, on my face, down my arms, even on my legs and feet. Mingling with the mud and sand from the mine. Tearing through the tourists with their tie-dye bedspreads and second-hand lamps. People stopping to gape in shock at the sight of me. Did you see the TV drama? Not much of a likeness I thought.

114

And after the funerals and the endless questions, after the policemen and the inquests, after the newspaper reporters and the psychiatrists — after they had all fucked off (no offence), still those looks, those glances, no matter how brief and how quickly disguised. Those quick, fearful eyes on me. That's why I asked to be moved here.

Maybe that's why I feel this way about Malcolm. He knows nothing about me, he likes the me of now, of today. I feel, Doctor Barton — I don't quite know how to put this — but I feel suddenly that there are possibilities for me. That there is a possibility suddenly of my life turning out a different way. That perhaps I do not have to stay thirteen, down there in the dark, forever.

★ ★ ★

Where was I?

★ ★ ★

When I left Patrick that afternoon and came blinking out into the street, I went to sit on a bench in the little park at the end of our road. For the first time in weeks tiny clouds peppered the sky and though it was still hot and the park was filled with smiling people and the summer sounds of car stereos and a nearby football game, I had the sense that summer was coming to an end. That something was coming to an end. I wondered where Kyle was, and what the fuck was wrong with him anyway. I wondered how I could face going back to school in a few weeks.

'Nit?' I looked up to see Esha and Bela. They were wearing cut-off jeans and bikini tops, each carrying a bottle of cider. They looked a bit sunburnt, dazed, drunk. They had grass all over them and had that flushed, soft-eyed look of people who have just been laughing a lot.

'What you doing, Nit?' asked Esha. They flopped down on the bench, one on either side of me.

'Want some of this?' Bela passed me her cider. I took a few big gulps, warm and flat and sweet.

'Easy!' she laughed.

'Aw fuck it. Let her get pissed if she wants.' Esha handed me her lit fag. 'What you doing out here by yourself?' she asked. 'Where's that little skinny mate of yours?'

I shrugged, took a drag of the cigarette and passed it back.

Bela nudged me in the ribs. 'He your lad, is he?'

'Fuck off,' I said. ''Course not.'

'Aw, I'm only messing.' She ruffled my short hair and gazed at me for a few seconds.

'Want us to do you a makeover, Nit?' she asked hopefully. Bela and Esha had been using me as a human GirlsWorld ever since I could remember. It had been a while, though — not since before Mum had died. It had been a torment when they'd come hunting for me with their make-up and glitter and Krazy-color hair-dye, but right then I kind of missed it.

'Nah,' I said though. 'You're all right.'

They got up then, already talking about what they were going to wear to the pub that night. Suddenly I didn't want them to go. I wanted to sit there for a bit longer with my sisters smelling of their Impulse bodyspray, of cut grass and cider and fags beside me in the sun. So I told them about Dad and Janice. Hadn't really meant to, just blurted it out. Told them I'd caught them 'doing it' and then I felt embarrassed. Should I have said 'Bonking'? I wondered. 'Screwing', maybe?

My sisters gaped at me open-mouthed then fell about laughing, clutching each other. 'Naaaaaaaaaaaah!' they said.

'Dirty old dog!' they laughed. They didn't seem to care, just wandered off home then, still giggling, with their cider, leaving me sitting there on the bench, feeling stupid.

★ ★ ★

Janice was round our house all the time after that, she practically moved in, and every time I looked at her I felt a bit sick. I cringed at her flabby belly, her loud laugh, the way she ate; stuffing it all in her gob and wiping her hands on her top. Hated her huge tits and her sweaty, orange-haired pits. She burped and laughed and spoke too loudly and took up too much room. She forced the fact of herself on you and I couldn't stand that. That's something I shared with Kyle, a hatred of the *disgustingness* of people. Do you know what I mean? I saw it in the way he looked at Denis sometimes, at the way he stared at Denis's fat wobbling when he ran, at the grunty noises Denis made when he ate. I recognised the look in Kyle's eyes; a little bit sickened.

And like me, Kyle hated to be touched. By anyone, I mean. Once, when I accidentally brushed my hand against him, he recoiled as if I'd burnt him. It's funny because I was the same. In some ways Kyle and I were very similar.

★ ★ ★

A couple of days later we went down to the river again. Kyle didn't say anything about what had happened at his house so neither did I. We went to the factory where the hideout was, then on to one of the big scrapyards. We loved going there. Piles and piles of cars in various stages of fucked. And mountains of twisted bits of metal, colours all faded and rusty, cool as anything.

It was easy enough to break into when there was no one there; you just crawled through a hole in the wire fence, but often there were blokes who walked around with dogs and who went spastic if they even noticed us hanging about outside and then there was no chance, we had to think of something else to do.

But that day it was empty. We found an old Mercedes and got in, Kyle behind the wheel, me next to him and Denis in the back. Some of the windows were smashed through and most of the leather of the seats had been ripped, big gashes pissing yellow foam. We ate Denis's bag of sherbet lemons, sucking them down until our mouths were cut to shreds and we could blow the fizzy gloop through the hole at the end, Kyle and I aiming it at the smashed windscreen in front of us.

Denis was talking to himself in the back seat, reciting from the A-Team, doing all the different voices, doing all the different faces. Endlessly, boringly in the stuffy heat of the back seat. First he'd do Murdock, 'Say, are we a groovy, happenin' bunch of guys or what?' then he'd answer himself in Mr T's voice, 'You been greezin' your head with battery acid again?'

On and on he went, I swear he knew every episode word for word. Finally Kyle turned to him and said, 'Stop being a fanny, Denis.'

'Damn fool,' said Denis quietly.

'Spastic,' said Kyle.

We talked about the castle near Greenwich Park that Kyle thought had a secret bunker in its grounds.

'I want to come with you,' I said suddenly. 'I want to come with you to look for it one night.' I just came right out with it like that. No big deal.

And he just shrugged and said, 'All right.'

It was so hot in that car. A fly buzzed drowsily in and out of the glassless windows and kept landing on Denis's head. Every time he batted it off it would buzz fatly away then return to land on his big, sweaty cheek or his ear or his glasses. He just kept flicking it away and eating his sherbet lemons. I could tell by the expressions he was pulling that he was still doing the A-Team, silently inside his head.

Then we heard the voices. Two men talking loudly to each other, arguing about something. They sounded like they were on the other side of the nearest stack of cars. The three of us ducked down and waited. The voices got nearer. I peeked above the window and saw two men standing 50 yards away from our car. They had the biggest Doberman I'd ever seen with them. 'Shit,' I said to the others. 'They've got a fucking dog.'

It started barking and straining at its lead, a frenzy of dribbling jaw and angry eyes and rippling muscle. It was looking straight at our Merc. So far the men were ignoring it. 'Shit-shit-shit,' I said. 'It knows we're in here.'

We heard one of the men say, 'Shut it, Tiffany, you noisy cunt' then carry on rowing with his mate.

'We'll have to make a run for it,' said Kyle. We looked over to the hole in the fence that luckily wasn't too far away, on the side where the dog and men weren't.

They had stopped arguing. We heard one say, 'Let's do a quick check round, then go and have a pint.'

As soon as they moved off and disappeared behind a stack of cars, Kyle and Denis opened their doors and keeping low, eased out. Then they legged it over to the wire fence. I was about to slide over to their side of the car and follow them but suddenly the dog was back. She had been let off her lead and was steaming after Kyle, a black, gleaming, rippling, barking frenzy of teeth and slobber and muscle. Kyle hadn't reached the fence and the dog was almost on him, its mouth inches from his ankle. And without even thinking about it I got out of the car, whistled at the dog and shouted at the top of my lungs, 'TIFFANY!'.

Scooby doo-like, the dog skidded to a halt and stood looking from me to Kyle, an expression of utter confusion on its face. 'Tiffany! Here, girl!' I shouted, desperately slapping my knees like a half-wit while Kyle threw himself at the hole in the fence. Suddenly the dog made up her mind and as she tensed and readied herself to fly at me the sight of her enormous mouth and the noise of her frantic, hysterical barking was almost enough to make me fall to the floor in terror, to make me give up and just let myself be torn to pieces, but instead I legged it round the other side of the car and over to the fence. Propelled by fear, I was over it in seconds, ripping my arm on a loose end of wire as I did so. I could hear the two men shouting furiously somewhere behind me.

Me and Denis and Kyle ran until we were back at our hideout, the three of us laughing so hard it was impossible to carry on. 'I love it when a plan comes together,' said Denis smugly, in his Hannibal voice.

Kyle stopped, gasping for breath, his eyes on me. 'Shit, Anita,' he said, and I felt overwhelmed suddenly by the way he was looking at me. The admiration was all for me, just for me. We both laughed, and I looked modestly at my feet, trying hard not to grin with pride. 'Thanks,' said Kyle, and I could feel his eyes on me still. 'I was almost Pedigree Chum back there.' He spoke softly and when I looked at him he held my eyes for a moment then leant across and to my absolute astonishment picked up my arm and examined my cut. I could hardly breathe. He frowned while he peered at it, then quickly let it fall with a dismissive 'You'll live.' I could only stand there, staring dumbly at my arm for a while, as Kyle and Denis wandered off, talking about something else.

We hung about in the hideout for a while, discussing the bunker at the castle, planning when we'd go there. Then we drifted towards the river and sat in silence for a while, watching some kids playing football on the shore below us. Eventually, Kyle asked Denis what the time was. Denis had a Casio digital watch his Uncle Richard had given him for his birthday. He loved that watch and was usually chuffed to bits when anyone asked him for the time. But right then he didn't answer. He was staring intently at a load of ants marching in single file over a lolly-stick by his foot, and he was oblivious to the rest of the world.

'Denis,' said Kyle again.

Nothing.

'Denis!' said Kyle, more loudly.

Nothing.

'Denis!!'

Nothing.

'DENIS!!'

Nothing.

'DENIS, YOU *SPASTIC!*'

Nothing.

Finally Kyle picked up an empty Lilt can from the floor and chucked it at Denis's head. It bounced off his short neat afro and he slowly came to, blinking in surprise.

'Who, me?' he asked, wonderingly.

'No!' shouted Kyle, suddenly so loud it made his usually quiet voice crack and both me and Denis jump violently. 'The other fucking mongoloid called Denis sitting on this bench.' Kyle's usually chalk-white face was red, his eyes bulging with a fury that had come suddenly from nowhere and I tittered nervously as Denis looked slowly from left to right, a baffled expression on his big moon face.

'Jesus-fucking-Christ, Denis.' Kyle thumped

124

the bench in irritation. 'You're a fucking-stupid cunt sometimes.'

Denis looked down at his shoes, while Kyle examined him from head to toe, disgust on his face.

'Look at the fucking state of you.' Kyle reached over me and spammed Denis on the forehead. Denis carried on staring at his feet. I froze, staring straight ahead and scarcely breathing. I didn't want him to start on me next. Kyle got up, went and stood in front of Denis where he sat, still staring down at his shoes. Kyle licked his fingers then spammed him again. Harder, this time.

'Come on, fatso,' he almost sang. 'What's the matter? Is Mummy's little sack of lard gonna cry?'

I looked at Denis out of the corner of my eye. Noticed he had tears welling in his eyes. I kept looking straight ahead, too chicken-shit to say anything. Eventually Kyle sighed, looked at both of us and shook his head. 'Man,' he said, 'why the fucking-hell do I waste my time with you two?' Then he walked off.

Me and Denis stayed sitting on the bench for a few moments, not meeting each other's eyes. Then we shrugged, got up and hurried after him. That was what it was like with Kyle. One minute he'd be laughing, the next he'd be going batshit about something. It was just the way he was.

As we walked, the sun began to fall and the shores lengthened in the twilight, nibbling and biting at the receding river. And as always at that time the freaks with their metal detectors emerged from nowhere in the dusk, scuttling across the muddy shores like welly-booted crabs, their machines whining, their silhouettes grey against the pinkly dying light. Only the gasworks were golden, caught in the last glow of sun where the river curved round in the distance. We stopped to lean over the railings to watch the treasure hunters, hating them. There was something intensely irritating about that army of idiots invading our beach, scavenging about in the muck and the filth for what? Some shiny piece of beauty, something important and worthwhile? Fuck off, we shouted silently, me Denis and Kyle. Fuck off, you'll find nothing here.

As we watched, Kyle said, blankly, angrily, not looking at us, 'My granddad wants you both to come round next Saturday.'

I remembered then, what Patrick had said. 'For your birthday!'

He didn't look at me, just said 'Yeh.'

We wandered off to the bus then, and he didn't say another word the whole way home.

8

It was a summer with no clouds and no breeze. A summer of melting tarmac and stinking dustbins, of five-pence ice poles and other kids on their front lawns, shrieking under sprinklers. A dried-up summer of glittering pavements and long black shadows. And the sun beat down without respite, every day the same. It was only Kyle who changed, only Kyle who shaped our days.

Days and days would pass where we'd just hang out and have a laugh. And when he was OK, talking about the caves, thinking up things for us to do, well like I've said, it was the best time of my life. I remember one time when we were up on Point Hill. The sun was just about to sink, the trees' shadows lengthening in the last light like a crawling tide. We were lying on our backs, looking up at the sky.

'When I grow up,' Kyle said, suddenly, 'I'm going to go all over the world. I'm going to travel to every country. I'll go to places like Borneo and India and I'll find caves and underground places that nobody else has dreamed of yet.' I turned to lie on my side, my chin propped up in my hand, and watched him talk. The evening up there above London was very quiet and sweet smelling and Denis and Kyle seemed more solid, more real than usual against the softly glowing sky.

Have you ever noticed how that happens sometimes, Doctor Barton? How in summer at twilight when the light is sad and vague, how objects and people are thrown forward; how the fading, dying light makes them stronger and more certain in the world somehow? It did that to my friends that night. I lay back and imagined Kyle in Borneo or India, discovering a cave, digging down bravely into the centre of the earth, a miner's torch on his head the only light to guide him.

'When I grow up,' said Denis, 'I am going to go to Africa to find my dad. I'll help him spread the word of God.' We were all silent for a while. 'Either that,' Denis continued, after some time, 'or work in a cake shop.'

'What about you?' Kyle asked me 'What will you do when you grow up?'

I lay there, Kyle on my left, Denis on my right, and thought about how I didn't want that summer to end, how I didn't want that moment to end. An airplane trailed gold above us. 'I don't know,' I said. 'I really don't know.'

But then there were the black days when Kyle would brood and stare and lash out at either Denis or me, or there'd be days when he'd barely speak and we'd just follow him about, our talk whittled down and wary while we waited for him to snap out of it, for things to go back to normal.

The day of the tramp, before the night of the mines, was a particularly bad one. I'd woken that morning hot and sweaty from queasy dreams of a seven-year-old me, of secrets and bad things, of my mother's tears and of waking up on piss-drenched sheets. The moment I saw Kyle on my doorstep my heart sank. You could almost see the shitty mood he was in like a dirty outline round him: a sick kind of Ready-Brek kid.

We knocked for Denis then went down to the river. Even he was quiet that day and in the shadow of Kyle's bad mood there grew between the three of us a pins-and-needles sort of atmosphere, a Chinese-burn sort of feeling while we waited to see what sort of turn the day would take. We found a dead rat on the river bank. 'Must have drowned,' said Kyle, kicking it, and we stood and looked at its staring eyes and black mouth for a while. But then Denis spotted the pissed old tramp from before, sitting above us near the jetty, so, leaving the rat, we went to watch him.

The three of us sat down a few benches away and Denis passed around the sandwiches his mum had packed for him that morning. The tramp was slumped over a bottle of wine, rowing with himself and carrying on, spraying spit and booze over his manky clothes. He reeked, even from that distance. Denis munched his sandwiches and stared intently at the old man. He was enjoying himself so much he let out a sudden roar of laughter, slamming his mouth shut like he'd caught a fly when the tramp turned to look at him.

'Gis one of them butties, son,' said the tramp. Horrified, Denis clutched his sandwich to his chest. I swallowed mine in one go and the tramp told us we were both a pair of cunts. He turned his attention to Kyle. 'Go on, son,' the tramp wheedled with his broken gob. 'I haven't eaten since yesterday. Spare a bit of grub for an old man?'

Kyle stared back at him black and steady as the dead rat and the tramp stopped shouting and stared at his feet. Then he said, suddenly and without slurring, almost like a normal, sober person: *You'll be like me one day, you little streak of piss.*

Straightaway I felt Kyle shrivel and tense

next to me on the bench and I held my breath. He passed me his half-eaten sandwich. 'Hold this and don't eat it,' he ordered, getting up, the look in his eyes making my heart sink. 'I'll be back in a minute.'

We waited ages for him. Our bench was right in the sun and I started to feel very hot. My head ached. Denis looked longingly at the sandwich but we both knew better than to eat it. The tramp shot us a few sulky glances but other than that left us alone. He began singing to himself, the words too blurry-crazy to make any sense. Finally Kyle came back carrying a blue plastic bag. 'Right,' he said, crouching down behind our bench. 'Give us my sandwich back.' I passed it to him. From out of the bag he took the dead rat and a bottle of bleach granules. Denis and I watched him take the top bit off his sandwich, and with his door key, saw open the animal.

'Yuk,' said me and Denis at the same time. The rat stank. Using the key, Kyle scraped out bits of its innards, red and green and black, wet lumps and globules and gristles, onto the ham and cheese. 'Looks like relish,' he grinned. Then he scattered on some of the bleach granules. Finally he put the top bit of bread back on. It didn't look very appetising but the tramp was pissed. And starving.

'Kyle,' I said. 'You've got to be joking.'

But he ignored me. I could have tried to stop him, I guess. I could have warned the tramp, but I didn't, I just watched. Maybe I wanted to see if he would really do it.

When Kyle reached the old man he leant down and said something I couldn't catch, then he passed him the sandwich, a pasted-on smile on his face. The tramp nodded at Kyle, then raised the sandwich to his mouth.

'Do something,' I whispered, to Denis, to myself.

Time seemed to stop. The tramp opened his mouth.

'Nooooooooaaaaaah!' It was Denis. He lumbered over to them, his hands clasped in the shape of a gun. He did a clumsy sort of roll on the ground like he was ducking sniper fire, then jumped up in the tramp's face, pointing his imaginary gun at him. 'Put the sandwich down, sucker,' he said in his Mr T voice. The tramp, his sandwich poised, gaped at him for a moment, then said 'Furroff,' and put the sandwich to his mouth.

'Aaaaah-SO!' Denis karate-chopped the sandwich out of the old man's hand. And the four of us stared down at the little mess of triangle-shaped bread, rat's guts, ham and cheese and bleach powder strewn across the walkway.

'Christ,' said the tramp, 'on a bike.'

We walked back to the bench, Denis stricken, Kyle white and knotted with anger.

'You could have killed him,' I said.

'Bollocks,' said Kyle. 'He's better off dead anyway.' He pointed at the stinking mess of beard and pissy rags and bones and wine bottle still sitting a few benches away. 'Look at him! *Look* at him! He's better off dead.'

'You can't do that, Kyle. You'll go to prison,' I said. 'You'll go to prison and I, I . . . ' *What will I do then?* I nearly said.

He interrupted, scornful and furious. 'Don't be stupid. It wouldn't really have killed him, just made him a bit sick, and he didn't fucking eat it anyway did he, so stop crying about it.'

'I'm not crying,' I said, the insult stinging me into silence.

Kyle shrugged. He wouldn't even look at Denis. Finally he turned on his heels and walked off back to Greenwich, and as usual, Denis and I hurried after him.

★ ★ ★

That was the night I found the old sand mine. I found it by accident. Ironic, isn't it, that it was the most important thing in the world to Kyle, the thing we'd been hunting for all summer, and there was me, literally just stumbling across it.

It was a night too hot to sleep and as I lay there in my bed I had the idea to go out exploring. Kyle did it, so why shouldn't I? And I thought it might impress him. I thought I might even bump into him down by the river. Then he could take me with him to wherever he was going. Just the two of us. And if I didn't find him, well then I could tell him all about it, and that might persuade him to take me with him next time he went out at night.

It seemed like a good plan, but as I lay there in my hot bed I felt afraid, suddenly, of the empty black streets and of the thought of me alone in them. I must have drifted off to sleep because suddenly I was wide awake, with just the vague memory of a door closing somewhere. I lifted the net curtain and peered out. Saw Kyle illuminated in the dreary yellow glow of a street lamp.

I got dressed in the dark, was outside in seconds, but even so he had already vanished. I hesitated and considered going back to bed, but the air was cool and sweet-smelling and I found myself walking in the direction of Greenwich. By the time I'd reached Deptford I hadn't seen a soul, just ghostly streaks of cars that flashed past me in the moonlight, and a squashed cat.

When I got to the river I stood looking over the railings at the water which was so high it almost reached my feet. The Naval College loomed behind me, its white stone floodlit a queasy green. It felt odd being there alone like that and the sense of excitement and adventure I'd felt on the way had almost gone. I imagined for a moment that I was the only person left on earth and the thought of it made me feel a bit panicky. The black river flopped and slurped below me and I wished that I was back at home in bed. I wondered where Kyle was, and though I wanted to see him I was anxious at the idea of him appearing, suddenly and shockingly in the darkness, so at the slightest sound I'd tense and look around for him.

After a while the sky lightened and I felt braver. I decided to walk further along the river to the hideout, to see if Kyle was there and by the time I reached it the river had turned a golden violet and the factory and its grounds stood in pools of red. I was wide awake suddenly and finding no one there, decided to keep walking.

I made my way through wasteland and vacant lots, filled with bushes of white flowers that in the warming air were already giving off a sweet and sour muskiness. I passed the gasworks and carried on through empty car parks until eventually I reached a scrapyard. It wasn't the one we'd broken into before, and I remembered Kyle talking about it once, saying it was a no-go because it was always guarded by men with dogs. I thought how cool it would be to tell him that I'd been in there, that I was brave enough to risk the men and the dogs in the middle of the night. All by myself.

It was surrounded by a high fence made from hardboard and corrugated iron topped with barbed wire, and I followed it round, looking for a way in. Finally I found a gap that someone had tried to cover up with chicken wire and planks of wood and I crawled through. We'd walked past the yard loads of times before and seen mountains of cars and mangled metal rising above the fences, heard men shouting and Radio One blasting from within, but now I realised that it was practically empty. They'd cleared it all out without us even noticing.

The place was massive. One lone pile of cars still remained in the far corner but apart from that it was just a vacant stretch of land with a few car tyres dotted here and there, a pile of empty beer cans and a forgotten hand-painted sign that said 'No Cheques, No

Credit, No Time-wasters, No Wankers'. I felt brilliant. I'd been brave enough to break in, but it turned out there was no danger at all! I imagined casually mentioning it to Kyle one day, saying, 'Oh yeah, that big scrapyard, past the gasworks? I went in one night, think it was about four in the morning, but there's nothing in there now.' Like I went out at night exploring all the time. Even Kyle would have to be impressed by that.

I sat on a car tyre and watched the empty yard turn from red to orange to yellow as the day began to gather strength. That's when I noticed the mound of earth and rubbish by the far fence. When I got closer to it I realised that it was odd, the way the ground just rose up like that, while the rest was so flat. Under some corrugated iron was a girder on top of a large piece of hardboard. I dragged the girder off and lifted the board to find a large hole. I couldn't work out what it was at first, thought that for some reason the scrap metal men had dug it, then I stuck my head in the hole and smelt the cold dank blackness and realised that the ground sloped down into steps cut into the earth, that it was the opening to some sort of cave.

God, I was so excited then. I'd found Kyle's sand mines, the ones he was always banging on about, I was certain that I had. I was torn between going in straightaway to see what was down there, and being too chicken-shit to do it without a torch. I thought about it for a while, then decided to go back to the hideout to get Kyle's. I rooted through Kyle's beaten-up old metal chest, dug around past his books and rope and penknife, found his torch and pulled it out, but just before I closed the lid, I saw something that made me stop. A rag doll, and beneath that, a little girl's red shoe. I knew immediately that they must be Katie's, knew that Kyle wanted to hide them there for some reason, but couldn't think of an explanation. Feeling confused and kind of guilty-excited that I'd discovered a secret of Kyle's, I shut the chest and left.

I ran the whole way there. There was still nobody about and I was glad; I'd been worried that I might bump into Kyle and I didn't want him to know about the mine yet, I wanted to explore it first then surprise him with it later.

I couldn't believe how ordinary the empty scrapyard looked in the sunshine: you'd never guess what lay beneath it. I shone the torch into the hole and wished suddenly that Kyle and Denis were with me. Finally I took a deep breath and on my hands and bum, I lowered myself down the forty or so uneven steps.

It would be easy to say now that the horror of what happened later affected my memory of how I felt that first time I went into the mine. But it's not true. I will never forget how awful it felt that first time, never. And the further down I went the worse it got. I was not claustrophobic and I had never been scared of the dark, but I felt sick suddenly and horribly anxious, like something was pressing on my chest. I immediately and very strongly felt like I couldn't bear being there and every instinct in my body told me to turn around and go back up to the sunlight. But how could I? It was the sand mine, it was Kyle's sand mine and I had found it first. So I told myself to get a grip and edged my way down further.

Finally I reached a small chamber about the size of two bus shelters. The walls were pale yellow and when I touched them they were dry and firm but with a strange powdery grittiness. Sand. My flashlight shone looming arcs on the ceiling. The coldness was immediate and shocking, it seeped right through you and made you long for the warm fresh air. There was a seeping bitterness in the air.

As the light from my torch swept over the

walls I noticed something that nearly made my heart stop. A huge grinning face with big, pupil-less eyes etched into the sandy wall, staring down at me. As I slowly turned and followed the light's beam, I felt my scalp prickle as I noticed more and more of them; all different sizes, some with no ears, some with no mouth, but all with those weird, blank eyes. In the torchlight the lines seeming to twitch and pulse in the hard, cold sand like veins under skin. And underneath each one a name: Mary, John, Bet, Tilly, Mark, Andrew. Dozens of names, dozens of faces. The effect was so creepy that I kept turning round and round flashing the torch everywhere to reassure myself that the people who had made those faces weren't hiding somewhere, malingering in the gloom. Looking back, that was the worst thing about it; the sensation that you weren't ever actually alone down there.

I remembered that Kyle had once told me that one of the Greenwich mines had been used during the war as an air-raid shelter and I imagined the people all huddled down there hiding from the bombs. I felt them waiting, frightened, in that tiny, glowing chamber, below the mental, banging, dying earth. All those people, etching out to pass the time those silent eyes that watched me now, waiting to see what I'd do next. It took every ounce of my will power not to leave.

The walls narrowed and then opened up again into an even bigger chamber, twice the size of the first one. I went in and sat on the floor, my flashlight casting yellow orbs on yet more faces. I realised, by its strange angle and unevenness that there had been some kind of collapse, blocking what were probably more caves behind. I wondered briefly if anyone had been down there when it happened. I felt breathless suddenly and no longer able to fight my desperation to get out. I scrambled back up the steps and dragged the hardboard and the girder back over the entrance.

The empty scrapyard looked exactly the same as when I'd left it, as if for the time I was down there the world had just paused and waited for me before it carried on turning again. The light hurt my eyes after the darkness. I felt almost hysterical with relief to be out of there and it took a long time for my heart to stop thumping. But on the way back to the hideout I told myself over and over how great it was going to be telling Kyle what I'd found. I kept picturing his face, how pleased and impressed with me he'd be, and I felt my spirits soar.

So why didn't I tell him for so long? I was going to, I meant to. But I guess I just decided that it was my trump card, I guess I sensed that I might need it one day. I never felt certain with Kyle, that he wasn't always about to tell me to fuck off and leave him and Denis alone. I was always afraid that one day they'd stop knocking for me. And when that day came, it would be good to have a bargaining tool; a reason to keep me hanging around. Besides, I'd never had something of my own before; I'd never had my own secret. Well, not a good one like that, anyway.

9

New Cross Hospital. 4 September 1986. Transcription of interview between Dr C Barton and Anita Naidu. Police copy.

I made myself look, in the end. With the lighter I could see Denis lying a few feet away. If I stretched my leg out I could touch his head with my foot. His neck was all twisted and his left eye was open and staring and the right one was shut. Above his eyebrow he had this big wound and I remember thinking that it looked a bit like a mouth with purple lips, the gleaming bit of bone poking through like teeth. There was dried blood on his face and in his hair and thick, black blood across his belly all over his Inspector Clouseau T-shirt, his favourite one, and his skin was too pale, it was much too pale. And further away, where it was too dark for me to see, there was another body. Dressed in pink, yellow hair.

The next Saturday was Kyle's birthday. I met Denis outside No. 33 and he banged the brass knocker on the huge black door clearly unimpressed by the grandness of the building that loomed above us. While we waited he worked his way through a kingsize bag of Maltesers, pouring them out into his pudgy hand and shovelling them into his mouth. Nobody came for ages then finally Kyle answered, a look of resignation on his face that said, 'Let's just get this over with.'

The same dank darkness of the hall, the glowing orange warmth of the huge front room, the same thrill I'd felt as last time. But now the oval oak table was covered in bowls of crisps and little sausage rolls, bottles of Tizer and an iced cake with candles. A few balloons lay scattered here and there. Kyle sat down at the table, folded his arms and stared stonily at his plate. Denis carefully rolled up his bag of Maltesers, put them back in his pocket and made a beeline for a bowl of Skips.

Across the room Patrick stood, bent over his pile of records. He smiled and straightened with a little grimace of pain and crossed the room in a few big strides when he saw us. 'Anita! How nice of you to come.'

I shrugged and muttered, 'S'all right.'

Patrick clapped his huge hand on Denis's shoulder. 'Always nice to see you, young man.' Denis barely looked up from his crisps. Kyle continued to stare down at the table and

I tried desperately to think of something polite and friendly to say.

At that moment Kyle's mum appeared. She stopped when she saw me and Denis. Just stood in the doorway staring at us, like she'd walked into the wrong house or something. I stared back at her. She was tiny but not how Denis's mum was tiny where you still felt she could do you some serious damage if she wanted to. Elizabeth was the sort of person who made you feel dangerous; one false move and you'd send her flying. She was a puff of smoke compared to the tightly wound spring that Gloria was. Darting grey eyes and fluttering hands that kept twiddling and pulling at her dress. Wrinkles and silver strands in her hair but more of a little girl than me somehow, more than I'd ever been. The sight of us all there seemed too much for her and she clung to the doorframe in bewilderment.

'Darling!' Patrick went over to her, took her hand and led her to the table, where he sat her down next to Kyle. It was funny the change in Kyle then. Even Denis looked up from his plate in surprise. Kyle flapped around his mum like a trapped bat, took her plate and piled it with sandwiches, picked up her shawl as soon as it fell from her shoulders and wrapped it around her. Anxious, watchful. Shocked, I sat down next to Denis.

Elizabeth said nothing while this was going on. Her big grey eyes stared at her teacup while her nervous little fingers pulled apart a sandwich. Denis helped himself to more of everything. Finally Patrick said gently, 'Lizzy, this is our neighbour, Anita.' I smiled, not knowing what to say. Elizabeth just stared at me, then finally managed a faint 'Hello.' Whispery and whispy. Her gaze drifted from my face and she relapsed into a staring silence.

'And you remember Kyle's friend, Denis?' She turned her eyes to Denis, who waved his sausage roll at her across the table.

Patrick put another record on then sat down with us and we ate the tea. He was jolly, chatting to me and Denis, asking us questions about this and that. Kyle said little, answering when Patrick tried to include him in the conversation, but mainly just staring at his mum.

I tried to follow what Patrick was saying but I couldn't take my eyes off Elizabeth either; her quick, nervous little movements, her little-girl's voice that had creeped me out so much the week before. Not that she spoke much; she was practically mute. She just sat, passive and remote, while the world spun on beneath her.

I wondered if she had always been like that or only since her daughter had disappeared. The way the three of them behaved with each other seemed so unconscious, so natural to them, that I sensed things had always been that way, that Kyle and Patrick had always treated her like a kid. It was like a kind of game, I realised, the point of which I couldn't fathom. I wondered about Kyle's dad and frankly couldn't blame him for fucking off to America, the woman was clearly mental. I didn't like her, wanted to shake her or throw something at her. Why? I wanted to ask the others. Why are you treating her like this? Like she's made of glass? Like she's six? But of course I said nothing.

When we had finished eating and Patrick had lit the candles on the cake and got Kyle to blow them out and we'd all clapped, he produced a small gift-wrapped package wrapped round and round with too much tape, and placed it in front of Kyle. 'For the birthday boy,' he smiled. We watched as Kyle unpicked it. It was a Swiss Army knife, red and shiny and heavy when you held it. The biggest one you could get.

Me and Denis went and stood by Kyle, took it in turns to hold the knife, weighing it in our hands. We watched Kyle take out all the blades; the little scissors, the corkscrew, the biggest knife and the smaller one, all of them — the little tweezers and toothpick too. He examined them one at a time while we watched admiringly, then he fanned them all out at once and there it sat, almost breathing, a gleaming red and silver insect in his palm.

I took it from him, I couldn't help myself. Gently I ran the biggest blade against my finger. So sharp and full of promise. One tiny bit of pressure from me and it would cut through the skin. Just one tiny push and there'd be blood. In that thin piece of steel the difference between feeling and not feeling, knowing and not knowing. It was beautiful.

Kyle took it back from me. A glimmer of pleasure and interest for the first time. 'Thanks,' he muttered to Patrick, then closed it up carefully, putting it in his pocket.

That was when Patrick announced Kyle's birthday outing. 'We're all going swimming!' he said.

Denis looked up from what he was doing, which was rubbing balloons up and down on his T-shirt for the static, then sticking them to his head. He stared at Patrick, appalled, as a green sausage-shaped balloon became unstuck from his afro and drifted slowly, dejectedly to the floor. 'Can't swim,' he said desperately, turning to me for back up.

I looked at Patrick in amazement. 'He can't, you know.'

But Patrick just laughed. 'Then it's about time you learned.' He began piling up the plates.

We looked at Kyle, expecting him to argue, but he had resumed his bored expression as if he'd just resigned himself to putting up with whatever was thrown at him that day. Elizabeth got up and wandered from the room. We all watched her leave.

Then, 'See to your mother, Kyle,' Patrick told him. A look, brief and unreadable, passed between them. It was like when your car goes under a bridge and it's suddenly dark and the radio cuts out. In a flash it had passed and Patrick's face was light and smiling again. Kyle scraped his chair back and followed his mum upstairs.

10

By the time they were thirteen my sisters were the stars of the Under-sixteens' Leeds County Synchronised Swimming Club. Like two, sleek, spangly costumed seals with matching swimming caps, when they paired off to perform their routine it was always the highlight of any competition. They'd do it to that Torville and Dean music, 'Bolero' or whatever it was called, and their perfectly timed scissorkicks, spins and lifts would have everyone in the audience cheering and clapping. Me and Mum would get the bus to whichever pool they were competing at and cheer and clap too, grinning at each other, knowing that those glamorous, clever water nymphs were ours.

They were the best times. Afterwards we would always do the same thing: go to a Wimpy for hamburgers and strawberry milkshakes. We loved going there. With its china plates and cutlery to eat your burgers with, and a Banana Sundae in a glass dish for afters, it was just like a proper restaurant. 'All girls together,' my mum would smile. They were good those days. The four of us — three girls with their mum — having a Wimpy tea and a laugh. My sisters happy to have my mum's full attention for once. Because they didn't, usually.

'Too wrapped up in each other, those two,' my Auntie Jam sniffed more than once, eyeing me and Mum disapprovingly. 'Unhealthy it is.' It's true my mum never let me out of her sight. The twins and Push mistook it for her loving me more than them, because they didn't know about my secret, the thing which only Mum knew and meant she kept me close to her, under constant watch, a necessary closeness that I suppose must have locked the others out at times. They just thought I was her favourite. That she focused on me out of love.

Me and Mum's secret. When she was dead the swimming galas and trips to Wimpy stopped, and so did her careful watch on me.

It was one of Bela or Esha's old swimming-club costumes that I took to Greenwich Baths. Patrick had to buy Kyle some trunks from the little shop by the entrance and he offered to buy Denis some too, but Denis said his mum had told him he could swim in his pants. I think that was the only time I ever saw Denis in a bad mood. He really didn't want to be there. He swung his plastic carrier bag with his towel in it and

151

stared longingly, sullenly, at the rows of chocolate bars and crisps in the vending machine near the ticket counter.

Me and Patrick were the only ones who seemed to be enjoying ourselves. To be honest I wanted to show Kyle's granddad what a good swimmer I was. On the bus over there I'd sat apart from the others and daydreamed that Patrick adopted me and took me and Kyle off to live in Scotland. I had never been there but I imagined green fields and lakes and little cottages with people like Patrick living in them. I knew I was being stupid but I liked imagining it anyway.

Greenwich Baths was old-fashioned. Victorian, Patrick said. It was all white tiles with little wooden changing cubicles along the edges like seaside beach huts. Above the pool was a gallery with rows of wooden fold-up seats. An onslaught of warmth and chlorine and echoey, excited laughter, kids running about and dive-bombing each other watched stony-faced by a blonde, pony-tailed lifeguard who sneered down from a chair on stilts, fingering her whistle like it was a loaded gun. A sign that said 'No Eating, No Bombing, No Running, No Fighting, and No Heavy Petting'.

We all followed Patrick up the nearest row of changing cubicles, but he stopped me and pointed over to the ones on the other side of the pool. 'Ladies are over there' he said. He said it nicely but I felt a bit stupid as I traipsed off on my own with my plastic bag. I squirmed into my sister's costume, careful not to look at myself, hurriedly pulling the pink stretchy material dotted with silver stars over the two little bumps that had only just begun to appear on my chest. I didn't want to think about them.

When I came out Patrick was already in the shallow end looking up at Kyle and Denis who were stood miserably on the edge of the pool. Self-consciously I joined them. Suddenly I saw us through Patrick's eyes: Kyle, shivering and scrawny, white and freckled in his brand-new, too-big trunks. Denis sulky and immense in his brown and mustard-piped Y-fronts and the orange arm-bands bought for him by Patrick. Me, a skinny brown boy in a baggy pink-and-silver one-piece. Not exactly contenders for the next Olympics, were we? But if Patrick thought we looked comical, he didn't show it. Just said briskly from the water, 'Come on now, kids. You're going to have to get wet sooner or later.'

I looked at Patrick, half-swallowed by the luminous blue water and felt a sudden stab of sadness. Without his clothes his shoulders looked a little puny, his chest a little frail. He reminded me a bit of one of those plastic inflatable chairs that have been sat on too often and have started to deflate and cave in. I preferred him buttoned up in his smart tweed jacket and stripy jumper. I noticed he had tufts of white hair sprouting from his ears, that his hands were covered in thick veins like tree roots. And although he still smiled brightly, I felt sorry to be seeing him like that, all wrinkly in the swimming pool.

I glanced at Kyle who was staring at Denis and was surprised to see a little smile on his face. Suddenly he elbowed me in the ribs. 'Look,' he said. 'Denis has got tits.' When Kyle laughed, which was rarely, he had this way of baring his teeth and snorting out of his nose; you could only be sure that he was laughing and not about to sneeze by looking at his shoulders. If they trembled and twitched it meant that somewhere inside he was pissing himself.

I looked at Denis and started laughing too. He did have proper girls' tits. At first I thought Denis was going to get the arse but he just grinned like he was proud of them and started doing a little dance to make them jiggle. The more we laughed, the more he jumped about until the lifeguard blew her whistle and fixed us with her depressed stare.

We got in, then. Me and Kyle jumped into the water; Denis climbed gingerly down the metal steps. He stopped laughing straight away, just stood with the water up to his waist, a look of abject misery on his face. Gently, coaxingly, Patrick began to demonstrate the breaststroke. Me and Kyle swam off towards the deep end, racing each other. As I swam (beating Kyle) I wanted to shout, 'Look, Patrick! Look at me!' but Patrick was too busy with Denis to notice.

Swimming is something I've always got very bored of very quickly. After ten minutes of going up and down, getting out and jumping in again, diving down to touch the bottom and so on, I'd had enough. Kyle was ploughing up and down still, his bony little head held stiffly out of the water and his two front teeth bared like a water rat's. I swam back to see how Denis's lesson was progressing. It wasn't. He was still in the exact spot I'd left him in. Patrick was imploring, 'Look, Denis, like this. Come on, son, give it a try, eh?' and making swimming motions in the air. Denis just stared balefully back at him, keeping his arms stubbornly raised at right angles so they wouldn't get wet.

When he saw me Patrick said, 'Anita! Come here and show Denis how it's done.'

When I reached him he put his arms under me as I floated on my front. 'Right,' he said. 'Pay attention, Denis. This is how you do the front crawl.' As Patrick supported me, I kicked my legs and chopped my arms. But Denis just got out and sat on the edge, his arms folded, his lower lip sticking out. He refused to look at us.

And suddenly Patrick was spinning me around, skimming me over the water, his arms supporting me under my belly. The pool flashed faster and faster around me. He kept it up for ages until I was dizzy and laughing and spluttering. Suddenly he stopped and lowered me down and I turned around, still getting my balance and waiting for everything to stop spinning and there was Kyle. Standing so close to us, only an inch or two away. When I saw his face the laughter caught in my throat.

'I want to go now,' he said, his voice dry and cold in that noisy splashing warmth. And then he just got out and headed off to the changing huts, leaving me and Patrick staring after him.

After I'd got changed I came out to find the three of them standing in the foyer. Denis had already bought a bag of crisps from the vending machine and was busy pushing coins in to buy more. We waited, while he frantically shovelled Monster Munch into his mouth with the desperation of someone afraid he might disappear if he stopped.

We walked towards the park, the four of us stinking of chlorine. It was getting late, the sky just on the brink of its evening transformation like a woman slowly, carefully, applying make-up. Little clouds appearing like dabs of blusher, streaks of pink lipstick smearing the sky. The light smells of blossom deepening into a more jaded, muskier perfume. We walked through quiet streets a world apart from the ones round our way. No old men leaning out of windows in their vests. No TVs blaring or gangs of kids on corners. Only wide, flat-fronted houses with window boxes and freshly painted doors. Expensive, shiny cars parked outside each one.

As we walked a lady and her daughter got out of a car, the woman's heels clipping smartly on the pavement. The girl had long brown hair to her waist, a pair of ballet shoes in her hand, the pink ribbons trailing from her fingers. She waited for her mum outside one of the houses and I must have been staring because as we passed she made a face at me, a wide-eyed Joey Deacon face as if to say 'What are you looking at?' And I ducked my head and hurried on.

As I caught the others up I wondered what

it must feel like to be that girl; to live your life in a big house and go to ballet classes every Saturday. When I was a really little kid I used to ask my mum, 'How do you feel?' When she replied, 'Fine, thanks, sweetie,' I would say, 'No, but I mean *how do you feel*? How do you *feel*, Mummy?' And she'd look at me and say, 'I feel fine, darling. Just fine.'

It was impossible to explain just what I meant. That my mum was a separate person from me hit me one day like a kick in the guts. That I couldn't and would never know exactly what she thought or felt, that there were secret, hidden parts of her I'd never be privy to, that I would never know how it really felt to be anybody else; not Mum, not my sisters, not the next-door neighbour who looked after me sometimes, nor anyone else in our street. I would never *know* them, feel what they felt. I was me and they were them and we were all separate and I was only five or something and didn't think it out in quite that way, it was more of a muddy fear, a confused jumble of thoughts. But as I grew older the idea began to overwhelm me, kind of. It wouldn't let me go — that sense of being so alone and unconnected in the world, of never being able to truly be another person, feel what they felt. I just couldn't ever seem to get past it.

I caught up with the others and we walked to the top of the hill. Opposite a little gate to the park was the castle Kyle had told me about, surrounded by high brick walls. The three of us stopped and looked in through the tall, black, iron gates at the wide, circular forecourt, the huge, arched wooden door and the blackened bricks of the turrets. Half a dozen cars were parked out front and from somewhere came the sound of laughter and music, the smoky wafts of a barbeque.

'Vanbrugh Castle,' said Patrick in a teacher's voice. 'Built by Sir John Vanbrugh in 1719. It was used as a school for years, but it's all flats now, I believe.'

We gazed in through the gates until a fat woman came out of the door, two Great Danes bounding beside her, and we slunk away. We walked on to the park and sat at the top of the hill, looking down at the royal palace below us. Patrick began telling us about the kings and queens who had lived there, how the park had been their garden, full of deer instead of tourists, when Kyle interrupted suddenly, abruptly, 'We're going down to the river now.'

Patrick looked at his watch. Smiled at Kyle and said, 'Well, OK, if you'd like.' Everything felt awkward suddenly. Kyle looked away, staring expressionless at the river that gleamed behind the palace. 'Well now,' said Patrick eventually, 'I'm sure you don't want your old granddad hanging about.' I felt sorry for him then, felt annoyed with Kyle for being so mean. I watched him get up stiffly, the cheerful wave and, 'Bye then. It's been a lovely day,' making it worse.

'Bye, Patrick,' I said. 'Thanks for taking us swimming.' I watched him walk off up the hill on his own. Turned to see a sneer on Kyle's face.

''Bye, Patrick,'' he mimicked. ''Thanks for taking us swimming''. He had my Leeds accent down perfectly.

'Oh, fuck off,' I said weakly.

'No, why don't *you* fuck off, Anita?' he said, his voice a dead weight. 'Why don't you just fuck off?' he said again, more loudly, when I shrugged and looked away.

'And while you're at it, why don't you just stay away from my house and my granddad?'

I stared down at my hands plucking the grass, waiting for it to stop, but he was working himself into a rage, I could tell.

'You don't fucking know anything, Anita. We don't want you. Patrick just feels sorry for you because you're such a skanky, stinky little Paki and your dad's an alky and your sisters are slags and you're poor and you've got no mum. He doesn't really like you and neither do I. Don't you ever come round my house again. I mean it, Anita. Stay away from my fucking house.'

Pain's a funny thing. Hard to describe once it's over, hard to recapture once it's gone. I think it felt like drowning might. His words filled me up like the muddy water used to fill up the Deptford Quaggy. And I felt it in my heart, it's a cliché but I really did. I felt my heart not break, not snap, but become saturated with his words, bloated with what he said until, too heavy, it sunk. I wanted to stand up and walk away but couldn't picture how I'd physically get up, how my legs would manage it. I looked at Denis who was watching us like we were something upsetting on the telly, like he was watching *Lassie Come Home* or something, the corners of his mouth turned down, his eyes all big and anxious behind his specs.

'Just shut up, Kyle,' I said. 'Leave me alone.'

He got up then. Kicked at the plastic bag with his towel and trunks in it, Denis's eyes following him agog. I looked at Denis rather than him in case I started crying.

'You're a fucking weirdo, anyway.' He was shouting now, a couple playing Frisbee turning to look at us. 'All you do is stare and stare. Never saying anything. Every time I turn around you're staring at me. Or you're staring at Denis, or I don't know, someone on the bus. You just fucking zone out and stare for ages. You don't even blink. Once I timed you staring at Denis for six fucking minutes. Your eyes go all funny. It creeps me out. You never speak, just follow us around. You do my head in.'

He stopped, then. Like he was all out of things to say. I almost laughed. Something almost made me laugh. Because despite the terrible things he was saying, despite how awful I felt, a tiny bit of me didn't quite believe him. Ninety-seven per cent of me felt annihilated, obliterated, but the rest of me sensed that he was acting. Putting on a show and hamming it up just a little too much. He was out of breath. His white little face pink around the edges. It was over.

I got up, finally, unsteady on my feet. Got up and stumbled off. Felt like I was sleepwalking. Felt like the contents of my head were falling through my body and were rattling around in my feet. Halfway down the hill I dimly heard him shout, 'Anita! Fuck's sake, Anita, come back.' And I turned, once, when I was at the bottom. Turned to see Kyle following me, far away. Denis jogging behind him.

11

New Cross Hospital. 4 September 1986. Transcription of interview between Dr C Barton and Anita Naidu. Police copy.

Last night I dreamed I was down there again, down there in the mine. Except this time I knew exactly what was about to happen. I knew what was going to happen but there was nothing I could do but wait for it. I was back there, listening to the girder being dragged, my heart going like the clappers as I watched the board slide away. I saw his face looking in suddenly all surrounded by light and I watched him lower himself down to where I was sat in the dark and I knew exactly what was about to happen next but there was absolutely nothing I could do to stop it. My screaming woke me up and I was too scared to go back to sleep again.

Can you believe, Doctor Barton, that my walk with Malcolm that Saturday morning five weeks ago was my first date? Twenty years old and having my first date! We didn't say much, not really, not that first time. Just walked over the suspension bridge then back again. Then we went to a café. It was difficult, because he didn't like to call the waitress over and neither did I so we both just stared at the table for ages before anyone noticed us and came over. He had chocolate milk, I had lemonade. He told me about his job at Speedy Gonzales. Then he told me what sort of films he likes. Sci-Fi is his favourite. Malcolm has a collection of Star Wars and Star Trek things in his bedroom but I haven't seen them because his mum doesn't like him bringing people back, and she especially wouldn't like a girl. They're worth quite a lot though he says. He's going to show me one day.

Mostly he comes round here. We watch telly on the portable that Push bought me. And when I'm with him, I feel like somewhere inside me, someone has turned the dial down from Freeze to 7.

★　★　★

Between Greenwich and Lewisham, behind all the estates, there used to run an alleyway so endless and creepy even Kyle preferred to take the longer route. It was getting dark, but it didn't stop me from going down it. I figured things couldn't get much worse for me that day, and I knew that if Kyle and Denis were still tailing me they'd be unlikely to follow me down there.

Still, it didn't take me long to wish I'd caught the bus instead. Long and bricked and narrow and winding and stinking of stale piss, the alley turned and turned for much longer than you thought it was going to. Just when you felt certain that a ten-foot murderer was going to appear around the next bend it opened out, finally, not to welcome, bustling streets but to a whole new level of creepiness.

It was a cul-de-sac, a cluster of prefab houses and shops which must have been meant for the estates, but then a Tesco opened up down the road and that was them fucked, I suppose. Everything was deserted and half-heartedly boarded up. Stuck in a different time. Like everyone had just been magicked away suddenly. Beam me up, Scotty. On the door of the Three Feathers a poster saying 'Sat nite is Disco nite'. Black and white pictures in Stacey's Unisex Salon of girls with 70s flicks, an ad that said 'Model's Required'. A grocer's and the newsagent, their iron shutters blocking out the years but through which you could still see a few forgotten tins of carrots, a charity box chained to the counter, some magazines still on the shelves.

In the twilight the street had a washed-out, faded quality, as if everything had been bleached the same shade of grey. The only bit of colour came from a child's abandoned jacket, its pink hood hooked over a bollard at the far end of the street.

I saw this drama on TV once about nuclear war. I watched it in the dark after everybody else had gone out or gone to bed and it gave me nightmares for weeks. As the opening credits rolled, a giant mushroom cloud rose above London, then a handheld camera snaked its way through a suburban street, into the kitchens and front rooms where bodies lay slumped across tables and over sofas or were lifelessly tucked up in bed. I remember the dressing-gowned corpse of this old lady, sprawled on her bathroom floor, a slipper dangling from her foot.

Walking past those houses and shops reminded me of that. I imagined dead families behind those boarded-up prefabs, a decaying barman behind the till of the Three Feathers, middle-aged women under the orbed hair-dryers, rotting beneath their perms.

The sky darkened and the lampposts glowed orange and I kept walking, concentrating on getting the fuck out of there and back into Lewisham as quickly as possible. And there

166

he was. Mike Hunt, the kid who wanted to kill us. Mike Hunt, leaning against a wall fifty yards ahead. It was turning out to be an *unbelievably* shit day. He hadn't noticed me and I considered turning back, considered walking back through the alley and taking the long route home, but there was something about the way he was leaning against the bricks, like one of those plastic spiders you throw at a wall, splat, and then watch it slowly dribble down again or like he'd been fired at the bricks by a giant sucker gun, his arms and legs at funny angles.

Then I noticed the blue plastic bag dripping from one of his fingers. Saw the nozzle of a canister poking out. Realised he was off his head and crept a bit closer, felt he was senseless to the world around him. And so I kept walking. If I hadn't things might have turned out differently. Doubt it, but they might have. I always think back to that moment, that split second when I decided to keep on walking instead of turning back (and what made me do that? Laziness? Recklessness? Fuck knows, fuck knows).

Anyway, I kept walking, and the closer I got to him, the clearer it was how wasted he was. I felt more confident then that he wouldn't even notice, never mind recognise me. I bent my head down as low as it would go, put my hands in my pockets and concentrated on being invisible.

'Paki,' he said, as I passed him. And he said it almost pleasantly, almost like a greeting. Like he'd just woken up and was pleased to see his old mate Paki there in the room with him. I couldn't believe how stupid I'd been. As soon as I heard his voice I realised; remembered what a psycho he was, that you didn't take chances with people like Mike Hunt, you did everything you possibly could to avoid them, even if it meant walking back down a frigging alleyway. I cursed myself at my stupidity and kept walking; felt, rather than saw him peel himself off the wall and stumble after me.

'Paki.' He was next to me then and I glanced up at him. His pupils huge in his pale-blue eyes. He put his hand out and stopped me. I felt the blood rush to my ears, the icy feeling in my spine. Tried to think what the hell I was going to do. We stood, looking at each other. He had a foolish grin on his face. It was almost childlike, almost sweet. But that expression kept floating away to reveal a harder, more focused one behind it. I noticed he had pimples all round his nose and mouth, shiny and yellow, saw how his skin seemed to creep and twitch over the bones of his face.

And behind the softly shifting conscious-
ness of his face, an evil in him like a metal
plate, like wire running through him. You
could almost see it behind those pale,
watery-blue eyes like broken glass in a kids'
paddling pool. I noticed that he couldn't
control his head properly, it bobbed about
and now and again his eyes would flutter and
you could see the effort it took for him to
remain focused and upright, but still that
hard glint of steel running through him,
always there, always sharp and ready for you.

I tried to move off and for a moment I
thought he was going to let me. He even said,
'Fuck off then, Paki, too fucking twatted
today anyway,' but just when I thought I was
going to get away, just when I thought I
was safe, his grip tightened. He peered at me.

'You!' he said. 'It's fucking *you*, isn't it?
One of the gypos from the bus?' He let go of
me while he stared, outraged. I tried again to
walk off and that's when he grabbed me by
the throat. Nothing wobbly about him then,
focused and lightning-quick he was. 'It *is* you,
isn't it?' he said, a slow smirk of pleasure
creeping over his face like an oil spill. He
looked down the street in the direction of the
alley. 'Where's your mates? The fat black one
and that bony little cunt?' When I didn't
answer he rammed me into the wall until I

said, 'I don't know. I'm by myself.' He looked at me more keenly then.

'Fuck me. Are you a girl?' The last word in shocked disbelief. I shrugged. He looked at me more closely, grabbed my chin with his pincer-fingers, waggled it back and forth. 'You are! You're a fucking girl. Shit, I thought you was a boy.' Wondering, reproachful, like I'd deliberately misled an old friend. He looked around him, checked there was nobody about, jabbed me in the crotch. 'Does your minge smell of curry, Paki?'

I tried to run, then. Pulled away from him, yanked away from him, fear biting at my throat. Tried to run, but he had hold of my arm. He was a head and shoulders bigger than me and I had no chance.

'Let's have a little look, shall we?' he said pleasantly. Then he spat, 'Fucking Paki bitch.' He dropped his plastic bag and I heard the clanking of his canisters. He held me against the wall by the throat with one hand, pulled at my jeans with the other. Ripped the top button from its hole, yanked at and finally pulled down the zip. My tears and snot were running down my face and onto his hand and he flicked it away with an annoyed 'Ew!' Then,

'Mike.'

It was Kyle. Just standing there. A metre

away. Just standing there calmly, come there to save me.

Kyle.

The relief, the gratitude, the pure joy lasted as long as it took to do my jeans up again and move clear of Mike, who was staring at Kyle with gaping, furious, disbelief. 'You!' he roared, and as he steamed towards Kyle and I saw the difference in them, the size of Mike compared to Kyle, the chemical-fired energy and strength in him compared to the quiet, tense smallness of my friend, the fear came back to me twice as strong; a useless, powerless terror as I realised that Mike was going to pulverise Kyle, then lay into me next.

And then, just as Mike made a grab for Kyle with one hand and raised his other in a fist, we both noticed the knife. The penknife, Kyle's birthday knife, opened at its biggest blade. Held in Kyle's hand which he raised, slowly and deliberately, stretching out his arm, the blade's tip inches from Mike's chest.

He backed away then, Mike. Lowered his fist. Stared — as if mesmerised — at the knife. His head had stopped bobbing finally. He was focused and alert now. At last he said, 'Are you fucking serious?' and shook his head in disbelief. 'What you going to do with that? Take us all camping?'

Still, he was unsure, I could tell. Kyle kept his arm steady, didn't say anything, just stared expressionless at Mike. And in those seconds while Mike made up his mind what to do, I had time to notice Kyle's eyes. Dead, they were, pure dead, like the time on the boat. Nothing behind them. He was off somewhere else, I could tell. A different fear, then, fear for Kyle, fear of Kyle, crept into my guts.

Mike shrugged, said, 'Fuck this shit,' made a movement to walk away then suddenly, quickly, turned back again, chopped his arm out to knock the knife from Kyle's hands, but Kyle was too quick and snatched his hand back then lunged, cutting Mike's wrist, neatly, cleanly, the blade slicing through the flesh, blood arriving immediately, thick and red, one wet, red drop falling to the ground. A sound from Mike, like a dog that's just been stepped on, then a furious, silent grab for Kyle's arm. But again Kyle was too quick and nicked him again, this time on the neck, just below the jaw. Blood again, but not so much, just a slow seeping redness, a thin oozing line.

Mike reached up, touched his neck, held his fingers smeared with blood to his face. Studied them, screamed, 'Fuck!' Went for Kyle again, kicked at him, shoved his trainer into Kyle's stomach and Kyle went down, but still he held the knife, he never dropped the knife. Mike kicked him in the ribs, went to stand on Kyle's hand but just in time Kyle reached up and stabbed him in the shin. Not just a nick this time, not just a cut, but a proper plunging, lunging, stab. I saw the blade disappear into Mike's jeans, heard him scream, the three of us staring at the knife eaten up by Mike's leg. Then Kyle pulled it out again, stood up.

Mike howling, hopping, holding his leg, pulling at his jeans, blood seeping out from under the hem, trickling onto the pavement. A red-black stain spreading across paleblue denim. 'Cunt!' screamed Mike. 'You fucking, cunting cunt. I'm going to fucking kill you. Both of you. I'm going to come after the pair of you with a fucking cleaver and chop both your fucking heads off.' Then he limped away, disappearing off into one of the estates, and we watched him go until we couldn't see him anymore, only hear his cries of 'Fuck!' and 'Cunt!' get fainter and fainter.

Kyle dropped the knife. Dropped himself, to his knees. Knelt there on the tarmac, his head bent. I picked up the knife. Wiped it on my T-shirt, closed the blade and put it in my jeans pocket. Sat on the kerb and watched him. We didn't speak, didn't need to. Just stayed like that for a minute or two. Then got up and walked home. Didn't speak the whole way back but I'd never felt so close to him. At his gate I didn't want to leave him, didn't want to be apart from him, but I stayed on the pavement and watched him walk to his gate by himself. When his key was in his door and I was moving off he said, 'Anita.'

I stopped, looked at him. His eyes were his again and he fixed them on mine as he said, 'We'll go to the castle, yeh? If you want to. We can go and look for that bunker.'

I nodded once, my eyes locked on his.

He looked done in, like he could hardly stand anymore. Like every word was an effort. 'I'll meet you here, outside your house at three,' he said.

I stared at him.

'Three a.m. If you're not here. I'll go without you.'

Again I nodded and he looked at me for a few seconds more, let himself in and closed the door.

12

At home, Dad, Janice and Push were gazing at Dennis Waterman giving George Cole some cheek on telly, fish and chips and a bottle of cider on the floor between them. Push was lolling open-mouthed on one of the brand-new easy-chairs he'd just turned up with one day in his mate's van. He said he'd found them on a skip which we all knew was bullshit but we sat on them anyway. He sprawled and squeaked restlessly on the shiny black leatherette. Cigarette smoke shifted in the hot muggy air like drifting snow.

Janice was sat on the sofa with Dad and her piggy eyes pinged open in surprise as I crossed the room to sit on the chair next to Push. 'You look tired, love,' she said.

'Yeh,' I said, staring pointedly at the screen.

'Busy little thing aren't you?' she went on, never one to be fobbed off easily. 'I was only just saying to your dad: don't see much of you, do we? Always out, always up to something.' She eyed me greedily for a while.

Dad glanced up, tried a smile, looked blearily back at the screen.

'See you with that Kyle Kite quite a lot,'

continued Janice. I didn't answer, just carried on staring at the telly. 'Funny boy, isn't he?' She examined her chipped nail polish. 'Never did really take to him.'

'I'm sure he'd be devastated,' I said under my breath.

'What's that, love?' asked Janice.

I shook my head and slunk further down in my seat but Janice whined on through the telly-noise and the mugginess.

'Used to see him and his little sister playing in the street. Poor little mite. She was always a treasure, used to wave at me when I walked past. Something funny about him, though.' She pursed her lips. 'Sorry, love, I know he's your mate, but to tell you the God's honest he's always given me the creeps. Those funny eyes of his.' She shuddered theatrically.

Nobody was paying any attention to Janice, even I was pretending not to. When I was little, I once pushed half a jellybean into my ear and couldn't get it out again. Janice's voice that night gave me the same sort of feeling.

'I remember this one time, not that long before the poor little love disappeared. I stopped to talk to her in the street, just to say Hello like and she was telling me all about her dollies. And suddenly that Kyle one just comes from nowhere, runs up to us and

176

yanks his sister's arm nearly out of her socket. 'Told you not to talk to strangers,' he's going. Then he pulls her back down the street and into their house and she's crying all the way. 'Kyle' she's going, crying her eyes out and I'm not surprised, he had hold of her that tight. 'Let go of my arm, you're hurting me,' she goes. Then he practically boots her through their front door.' Janice wrinkled her nose and nodded her head decisively. 'No, nasty piece of work that one. You best stay well clear, love.'

I continued staring at the TV and finally Janice gave up and stopped eyeballing me. The room's stuffiness and TV sounds coated me like warm oil and I felt myself sinking into something like sleep. But shifting in my seat, I felt suddenly the hard weight of the penknife dig against my thigh. Instantly I saw again the blade touching then piercing Mike's flesh; replaying in my mind was the blood, the dead grey stare of Kyle's eyes. And I thought back to when I'd first held the knife in my hands and had run the blade across my own flesh, how the steel and red plastic had gleamed and trembled in my palm.

I thought of Kyle's face and then without warning came the sickly sliding thoughts I hadn't had since I was six. They came creeping, seeping through the sleepy fug, and then came the slicing heat behind my eyes. I couldn't help it. I couldn't stop them from returning. After all those years, suddenly there they were again, unwelcome guests at a crap party. Old enemies reneging on a long-held truce.

★   ★   ★

'I'm off out.' Jarred awake, I stared dumbly after my brother as he slammed out of the house, then down at a plate of beans on toast, grown cold, placed there on the arm of my chair by Janice, minutes or hours before.

I went to bed early, slept immediately; a thick, muddy sleep from which I woke to the sound of gravel on my window. Alert and panicky suddenly, I looked at the clock: 03.06 a.m. 'Shit!' I said out loud and heard Esha murmur a sleepy response as I grabbed at the net and looked out into the street to where Kyle stood, staring back at me. I pulled on my clothes and was out of the door and next to him by seven minutes past.

A nod, a look, something understood. That walk, that long, dark walk to Greenwich the best, the happiest, the surest I'd ever felt.

It took us almost an hour. Through Brockley, down to Lewisham, up to Blackheath. On the way the yellow streaking flash of night buses, a few, grey, shadowy forms inside; a shouting puddle of piss-drenched rags in a doorway, a woman running, crying in high heels, but mostly silence, mostly dark, warm silence. And then the heath stretching out, moonlit and flat before us, the lights of London singing below.

I remember we didn't really speak on the way — I remember because when Kyle did suddenly say something it made me jump to hear his thin quiet voice, like a mosquito landing on still water. He said, as if it had just occurred to him, and like he wasn't really that interested, 'So, where *is* your mum, then?'

'Dead,' I said, too surprised to elaborate. He nodded as if my answer satisfied him completely and I felt encouraged to ask him a question of my own, though as soon as I'd said it I felt reckless and clumsy.

'Your mum,' I said, watching for his reaction. 'Why's she, so . . . you know?'

He didn't answer right away, and we walked on for a few minutes in silence. I was sure that he was angry, and I braced myself.

But, 'She's delicate,' he said finally. 'Granddad says we need to look after her. He says she's not . . . ' he paused, searching for the right words. 'She's not very well.' It was a vague enough answer but still it made me feel a little queasy, because the way he said it

179

reminded me of a little boy reciting something drummed into him long ago. 'Her nerves couldn't take it.' He added as if that explained everything. Although what 'it' was, he didn't say.

I thought of the three of them in that big old house, of Kyle and Patrick tending to Elizabeth like she was a sickly child, stepping around her softly as if around a cut-glass vase, and I shivered. A picture popped into my head of a straw doll, and Patrick and Kyle with burning matches in their hands. I felt like I should say something in response and thought about cracking a joke about his family being almost as mad as mine, but decided against it. We walked on in silence for a while until I could bear it no longer. I had to ask him. And a part of me listened in disbelief to my voice as it spoke the words.

'What happened to your little sister, Kyle? What happened to Katie? You know, don't you?'

A sudden intake of breath and a sharp turn of his head to look at me then quickly away again and I closed my eyes, stealing myself for his fury. His voice, when he spoke, was like the strike of a match. 'Mind your own business, Anita.'

I nodded, not looking at him, miserable for bringing it up, but then he stopped walking.

We had reached the main road that slices through the heath and under the glow of a street lamp we faced each other. He looked at me in silence for a while, then opened his mouth to speak but seemed unable to get the words out, a look in his eyes like someone trying to push a car uphill. Without thinking I reached out and touched him on the arm. Said, 'What is it, Kyle?' and he flinched from me. 'Sorry,' I said, in agony by then, and put my hands in my pockets out of harm's way.

Again he tried to speak, but could only manage a splutter, little drops of spit flying from his mouth like pins. In the lamp light his eyes like knives. 'I,' he said. 'I . . . '

'What?' I whispered.

We stared at each other.

'Just fuck off,' he shouted and I jumped out of my miserable skin. He crouched down suddenly, his head in his hands.

'Kyle,' I said, close to crying. 'Kyle, please don't.'

Tears in his eyes shocking me into silence.

A night bus passed, its only passenger swivelling to stare down at us from the top deck. Still Kyle crouched there and I knew he was oblivious to my presence. I reached out and touched his shoulder and this time he didn't react at all, so lost was he. He stayed there, clenched tightly away from everything and as my hand rested on his shoulder suddenly the feelings from before, from another life, the feelings I'd almost managed to forget, came back so strongly I almost lost my balance. They flooded my mind and I backed away from him.

Kyle straightened up at last and pulled himself together. 'Just mind your own *fucking* business,' he whispered. And we walked on.

*   *   *

At the gates of the castle we waited, listening to the barking of a dog. Then we followed the high brick wall around until it disappeared into dense shadows and trees. 'Over here,' said Kyle by its lowest point and we pulled ourselves up and over into the garden on the other side.

We found wide lawns bathed in moonlight and the castle looming black against the dirty orange sky. We ran from it, towards the edge of the grounds, past children's swings and roundabouts and a pen full of sleeping goats. 'Here.' Kyle stopped by a high wire gate in a fence and I saw that below us the ground dropped away steeply and there it was: a sunken forest. Black and damp; quivering, almost breathing in the darkness.

A secret forest by a castle. It sounds like

fairy-tale bullshit but it *was* there, still is, I expect; nestling amongst the big town houses and carefully manicured gardens of Greenwich like a guilty secret. A sunken forest about the size of two tennis courts that you had to scrabble and slide down a muddy slope to get to.

Kyle switched on the torch he had brought with him, because there, under the trees, it was pitch-black. Slowly we moved between the trunks and through vines and weeds and dead leaves, following the beam. There was a damp and heavy coolness that I hadn't even known I'd been longing for all those weeks. Neither of us spoke. I felt like we were the only people left in the world. Or like we were on our own planet, spinning a billion miles away from the confusing, relentless light of earth. I will never forget that, the two of us walking there together. I don't think I had ever been so happy. We were so close, so at ease with each other. I didn't want it to end and I think he felt the same way too. Our friendship seemed to stretch out into the evening and fill every corner of that cool, dark place.

And then, 'Here.'

Kyle was shining the torch into a clearing and as we got nearer I saw that at the end of his beam the earth rose in a low arch. I felt the air around us tremble and stretch with Kyle's excitement as he began to pull away bracken and branches to reveal the opening of a bunker; stone steps leading down to blackness.

I followed him down to an arched, brick chamber, it had a musty, sweet smell, a dry warmth. 'I wonder what it was for?' I asked, breaking the silence. But Kyle didn't answer. We sat on the ground for a while and I felt his happiness there in the darkness, under the sunken forest, under the world. I didn't tell him that I wasn't that impressed — it was just a small, man-made cellar after all. But I let him have his satisfaction. Kept quiet about my secret. There was better, deeper, bigger, I knew. I already knew there was, although I hadn't yet told Kyle.

He turned the flashlight off and we sat in silence for a while. The easy, warm feeling between us seemed to deepen there in the darkness. Finally he said, 'Anita?'

'Yeh?' I said. He was silent for a moment or two. I heard his breathing become ragged and realised he was crying. I didn't know what to do; I dared not risk touching him again. 'Kyle,' I said. 'Kyle, what is it?' He didn't answer, and I listened to him gasp in the blackness. After some time he said, 'It was me. Anita. It was me,' and his sobbing became so loud and desperate suddenly that I reached out and felt for his arm, but when I found him he pulled away.

'*What* was you, Kyle?' I asked, desperately. 'Tell me. Please, tell me what you mean.' But he wouldn't say another word, and gradually his sobs subsided and he was quiet. Minutes passed and finally he said, so quietly I had to strain to hear him, 'I want to stay here for a bit. On my own.'

All right,' I said. 'I don't mind.' And I didn't. I understood. I heard him put the torch down and curl up, his breathing becoming more steady and shallow.

'Come out before it gets light,' I said. 'You don't want to get caught.'

I left, finding my way back in the dark to the wire gates, then running back across the moonlit lawns.

I went to Point Hill. I sat on the bench in the little park that overlooks the city and thought about Kyle sleeping down there under the earth, the need in him to be deep beneath the traffic and river and houses and people. To hide far below the world with all its noise and fury. I looked down at the valley of lights and thought again of the blood pouring from Mike's leg, Kyle's dead, grey stare as he plunged the knife into denim and flesh and Mike's incredulous screams. And

185

the question that had always been there, the question I'd never dare ask again. What had happened to Katie, all those months ago? Where was Kyle's sister now?

★ ★ ★

I pulled the penknife from my pocket, opened the biggest blade and stroked the shining steel. I looked up at the stars which held the sky in a vast and brilliant net despite the pink light beginning to bleed from the horizon. I soaked up the immensity of the city below me and I felt such a sudden strength and power and happiness I stood up on the bench and raised my arms above my head. I felt myself soar over London, swooping down from Point Hill over the lights shining from a million naked bulbs. A million headlamps from a million cars moving between a million streetlights. And as I stood there a million keys turned inside me, a million doors suddenly opened.

There, high above London I felt my heart connect with Kyle's sleeping far below me. And I flew above the city, his protector, the blade in my fist.

13

He didn't speak to me, I guess he just wanted to get on with it. He left the hole uncovered and I could see the rock in his hand and I could see his eyes but it must have been harder for him to see me, you know what I mean? For his eyes to adjust to the light and that, because he never saw the knife in my hand. He never saw the knife. When he found me he lifted up the rock to slam into my face, to finish me the same way he'd finished the others, and without even aiming at his throat, that's where the knife got him. I had to. I had to kill him before he killed me. And afterwards, I didn't run immediately. You'd think I would, wouldn't you but I didn't, I just sat with them lying all around me, and the sun shining in on them through the hole and it was so quiet, so completely quiet. I sat there for a little while because I knew that as soon as I got up, as soon as I got up and ran and left them behind it would all be real. Do you know what I mean? As soon as I left the mine the future would start and I would be the person that this had happened to and there would be no way back. So I sat there with my friends for a few moments. And then I got up and I just ran.

Malcolm has light-brown eyes and when he looks at me I feel happy-panicky. Excited-sad. Two weeks ago we went to our café again, and on the way there he picked up my hand and held it. I just froze, Doctor Barton. My mind went blank with panic. I shook his hand off and ran away. Just left him there in the street. Can you believe that? Ran all the way back home and didn't answer the door when he knocked. He kept coming back all afternoon, kept knocking. 'Please,' he kept saying, through the door. 'Please. I'm really, really sorry, Anita. Please. Anita, please.' But I didn't answer, and finally he went away. We were supposed to be going to the cinema that night.

But you don't want to hear about that, do you, Doctor Barton? You didn't come all this way, write me all those letters just to hear about Malcolm and me. No, you wanted a catch-up, didn't you: a little reunion with your favourite patient.

* * *

It wasn't my fault. None of it was my fault.

* * *

I didn't see Kyle for two days after the night of the castle, and I thought I'd go mad, I was so desperate to talk to him. I'd started to feel like things didn't really make sense when I wasn't with him, like I didn't really exist if he wasn't around.

By Tuesday afternoon the waiting was driving me nuts. I stood for a while by our front-room window just staring out at his house, waiting for him to appear. After a while I went and sat on our front step. I thought about how school would be starting in a week, how all the streets and buses would be filled with kids in uniform, me amongst them. A faceless stream of children all dressed the same, all looking the same. That day I was wearing a pair of Push's shorts and the sun was beating down on my knees. I covered them with my hands and the sun bit into them instead. I stared across at the big black door with the two threes, willing it to open.

After an hour I told myself to stop being stupid and tried to make myself get up and knock on Kyle's door. But I couldn't do it. I kept remembering the time in the park, when he'd shouted at me and told me to stay away from his house. I knew that things had changed since then; I knew that everything was entirely different between us now, but still I couldn't quite face it. That's when I remembered the penknife. I still had it. It was upstairs under my mattress. Kyle's birthday present. Surely Patrick would ask Kyle where it was? Surely Kyle would want it back? He'd want it back right away, wouldn't he? Course he would.

I ran upstairs and was back in seconds. Hesitated for only a moment, then went over to Kyle's before I changed my mind. Up the four steps to his door, my hand on the knocker, then I stopped. It was open. The door was ajar. I stared at it like a moron for a few moments. Then knocked. The door shifted open another inch. I waited. Nothing. I put my ear to the gap and listened. Nothing. I peered in, nudging the door another inch. Nobody. I knocked again, waited, then went in.

I pulled the door to behind me and stood listening to the house. It was completely silent. I strained my ears but couldn't hear a sound, not a tick or a drip or a murmur or a creak. I wondered if they had all gone out, and panicked slightly at the thought of the three of them returning suddenly and finding me there — an enterer if not a breaker, but practically a burglar, standing on the wrong side of their front door. Then I remembered Kyle's useless mother and her inability to leave the house, and I guessed they must all be upstairs, tucking her in and reading her a story or whatever the hell it was they did with her. I almost left.

Almost.

I didn't want to call out; I wouldn't have liked to have heard my voice echoing up those silent stairs, and anyway, I was too afraid of Kyle finding me stood there in his house like that, uninvited and unwelcome. I shuddered at the thought of it. I made up my mind to leave, to continue my watch from the other side of the road, to wait until Kyle returned from wherever he had gone. But I didn't. I didn't because at the end of the hall, past the lounge door, was a room I'd never been into. And it was just way too tempting. Have you ever been in somebody's home when they don't know you're there? You should try it; it's fun. I decided I'd just nip down the hall to take a quick look. Just a quick one, then I'd leave. Definitely. No harm done. Like I've said, that house was fascinating to me.

The room turned out to be their kitchen, and it was almost as big as the lounge. It had battered red tiles on the floor, a big white trough of a sink filled with dirty pots and plates, an old dresser piled high with random crap you don't usually find in a kitchen: a fur hat, a stack of books, a roller skate. The table was covered in dirty plates and half-empty cans of food. Someone had dropped their toast on the floor. A fucking mess, in other words; it made my house look good.

Disappointed I turned to leave, but then, out of the corner of my ear, I heard a noise. It was barely there. It was like a sound heard in your sleep, a sound you're not quite sure you really heard, more of a shift in the air than an actual noise. And then I heard it again. For the first time I noticed a door at the far end of the kitchen. I noticed that its opaque glass panels had little flowers cut into them and they twinkled and winked their invitation. I had a quick look over my shoulder before going over to peer in.

And there they were: Kyle and Patrick, in a tiny, low-ceilinged room that I guess must have been some sort of outhouse. There they were, caught within the confines of my petal-shaped spy-hole. I saw them in that little room that like the kitchen was full of crap, saw them bathed in a golden light that seeped and creeped into the dusty air through dirty windows. I saw them. Like an old-fashioned sepia photograph; a silent yellow-tinged moment, suspended forever, indelible, undeniable. I saw them.

The top of the window in that little room had a stainedglass panel and the sunlight threw red, blue and green squares on Kyle's naked back as he stood, his face hidden in his grandfather's embrace. And nothing moved, nothing moved at all; not me, outside looking in through the petals, not Patrick, his eyes closed, as he sat on a rickety old table, his trousers and underpants bunched around his feet, his wrinkly hand its veins like roots caught in green light across his grandson's bare buttocks.

Nothing moved at all in those seconds while I stood somewhere I shouldn't have been, in someone else's kitchen, staring through a glass daisy on a sunny Tuesday afternoon, the summer I was thirteen. Nothing moved, everything was still, except for my friend's hand which shifted back and forth, back and forth, not quickly not slowly but carefully, deliberately, in his grandfather's naked lap.

★　★　★

I felt my guts shrivel then splinter.

The world fractured, it let go of me.

A million flecks of light filled my vision, adrenalin shot through me like I'd missed a step on the stairs and I was falling. I kept on falling. Looking back, I guess from that moment on I never really did reach firm ground again.

I backed out of the kitchen, my feet like they had people tethered to them and somehow made my way into the hall, almost made it to the front door.

Almost.

Because there she was, Elizabeth. Halfway down the stairs she stood, one hand on the banister, one hand to her mouth. Frightened, guilty eyes darting from my face then over her shoulder to the kitchen door. Frightened guilty eyes telling me that she knew, telling me that she'd always known.

14

A red car's bumper grazing the backs of my knees, some old doris behind the wheel, her face blank, almost serene with shock. The noise of her horn competing with the screaming in my head. A bloke in a green tracksuit, him and his dog both frozen in slack-mouthed amazement. The door of No. 33 wide open still. The sun shining on my face. I wondered for a moment if they were in on it too, if the whole fucking world had known apart from stupid, stupid me, and then I realised that I'd almost been run over, that I was standing in the middle of the road. That was all.

The man with the dog was saying something, his words floating between us like smoke. He started walking towards me and the old bird was getting out of her car. So I just turned and legged it until I got to the park at the top of our road. I sat on a bench with my head almost in my lap, vomit in my throat, wishing I could burrow through the grass and the earth and the worms and the roots and curl up there where nobody could find me, and I understood then why Kyle wanted to, knew then what he meant. But instead I just sat there on the bench and listened to the knives sharpening in my head, the taste of metal in my mouth.

★ ★ ★

It was dark when I got home. Everyone was in, even my sisters. The sudden noise and brightness from our front room like a face-full of acid after the quiet of the park. I tried to slip past the lounge door and up the stairs but then there they all were: Esha and Bela and Push and Janice and Dad, crowding out into the hall, ten excited eyes on me like teeth. I thought I might faint so I leant against the wall to stop myself from falling. I tried to focus on the bit of white paper Janice was waving in my face.

'Bem Bom Brothers,' she was saying. 'Margate!' she said. Her pink-frosted gob open in a wide excited grin, a crowd of tiny yellow teeth like tic-tacs. 'Fun fair.'

I looked at Push who was feigning boredom. 'She won it,' he said. 'We're all going to Dreamland.' And then he smiled like he was six again.

They all started talking at once. Something about a raffle, something about Janice's sister who worked at the local spastics home and she'd fiddled it so Janice had won, and they were all going and did I want to come to Margate to ride the Scenic Railway and maybe the Mary Rose? Train fare there included, all the rides too. Did I want to? Make a family outing of it?

Yeh, I said. OK, I said. If it meant that I could go upstairs. If it meant that I could sleep.

*   *   *

Lewisham station, platform two.

Everything unclear, like looked at through water. Random stuff thrown suddenly into focus. Graffiti on the wall, 'Michelle loves Jon' and 'Darren bumfucks packys'. A puddle of Tizer by my feet from a long-gone stranger's spilt can, which I stared at and stared at like it was one of those religious miracles, like when thousands of people travel across the world to see God in a damp patch or Jesus on a piece of toast. Like if I stared long enough I'd see something in it that made some sort of sense.

Seeing only Kyle's arm moving between his granddad's naked thighs.

The six of us waiting for the train to come. We'd all got up specially early and the heat by nine a.m. was extraordinary, the hottest it had

197

ever been, as if the sun was giving one last blast, one last gasp before imploding.

'Did you know,' Kyle had said once, 'that the sun is shining itself smaller? That the more it burns, the smaller it gets? Every day the sun shines, it weighs a little less. One day there'll be no sun at all.'

I thought of Katie Kite. I thought of Kyle's mum's face when she saw me in the hall. My head a pinball game, the thoughts ricocheting off the sides. I started to hear a noise like someone running a stick along railings. Realised it was inside my head.

Me standing in Kyle's front room with Patrick.

'*What did happen, Patrick? What did happen to Katie?*'
'*I don't know, my dear. I really don't know.*'

The train came and we all got on. A single compartment. Do they still exist? Our own private carriage, stinking of hot dust and stale fags, the seats covered in green and red bristly stuff. The floor the colour of Kyle's eyes. The white shiny walls smeared in something brown, something yellow. A swastika and an NF sign next to a giant penis with three little drips shooting out of

198

the top in blue biro. 'I love you' underneath in black. Me and Bela and Esha on one side, Janice and Dad and Push facing us. No light bulb, so we sat in darkness when the tunnels came.

Janice wore a dress, pink and shiny as a Wham bar. Her boobs like bald men's heads. The sun followed us through the open window and I kept slipping in and out of hot sleep. I listened to Esha and Bela's conversation, heard how their Yorkshire accents had morphed without me noticing into a south-London West Indian twang.

'So he goes, you're a slapper, and I says, nah fuck you man.'

'Naaaaaah?'

'Yeah mate.'

'Uh-aah! Bwoy. Cheek of him!'

'Innit?'

★ ★ ★

I thought about the night I walked to the castle with Kyle.

'What happened to your sister, Kyle? You know, don't you?'

Kyle's face, yellow in the lamp light. My hand on his shoulder.

I sat up straight, shook my head, tried not to think of anything at all. My eyes felt sore and everything seemed unnaturally bright, like it had been scribbled over in yellow highlighter pen. I stared hard at Push just for something to do. He was gazing out the window listening to a Walkman he'd come home with one day, saying his mate had given it to him (though it was brand new and still in its box) and I noticed for the first time a Nike swoosh he'd had shaved into the side of his head, saw too that he had hair sprouting from his top lip. Noticed how his fingernails were bitten down to the quick, and most of the skin on his fingertips gnawed away too. Ten raw and scabby stumps, one of them wearing a big gold ring. The sight of them for some reason making my chest tighten. Then we went into another tunnel, and came out the other side.

I felt the walls of my mind begin to close in on themselves.

Dad and Janice each cracking open a can of Co-op lager. My dad in his cardi, touching cans with Janice, saying 'Cheers.'

Kyle's arm in Patrick's naked lap.

Suddenly Janice was squeezing herself in between me and Esha, lager slopping onto her knee, a look of concern on her fat caked-on face. I realised from somewhere far away that she had been talking to me for some time.

'You all right, lovey?'

Patrick's trousers around his ankles.

I stared back, trying to focus.

'Yeh, I'm fine.'

She held a sweaty, pudgy hand to my forehead. Eyed me with distaste. 'Don't like the look of you, sweetheart.'

She turned to my dad, who was watching us with a shy smile. I put my head in my hands and tried not to cry. Pulled myself together just in time.

'I'm fine,' I said. 'Just hot.' But Janice had turned away and was talking to Push about something else.

We had to change trains twice before we reached the Kent coast. We walked from Margate station through the town towards the beach, carrying the plastic bags which held our sandwiches. The sun hung heavy in the sky and the world shrunk and burned under it like a hot, sick dream. We trudged past shops, the ones that weren't boarded up selling ice cream and giant candy dummies and beach balls and buckets and spades and hats and fake tie-on boobs and hoola hoops and plastic tennis racquets and the streets were crazy with people and when we got to the beach everything was bright, so bright it hurt my eyes.

And I thought I'd never seen a sky so big. We walked onto the beach like we'd just landed on the moon, the sand burning through our flip-flops. I trudged behind my family, not thinking or feeling or seeing or hearing, just stopping when they stopped, walking when they walked. Heat and people and sea gulls and noise and wide blue sky and then there was the sea and I stopped and stared because I'd never seen the sea before, and I wondered which bits of it had once been in the Thames. Its vastness, its endlessness, making me feel suddenly panicky, like a trapped bird was flapping its wings inside my chest. We stood, the six of us, all in a row along the sea shore, looking without speaking, just staring at the waves.

Then a screech from Janice. 'Look!' and we all stopped and followed her finger to where she was pointing and there, at the end of her finger, at the end of the beach, a roller-coaster loomed high against the vast blue sky and then we noticed the entrance gate which said 'Bem Bom Brothers' Dreamland' in flickering lights on top. I looked at my family's faces all squinty and pleased, staring at the gates to the fairground, like all the answers to all their dreams did indeed lie behind them.

Dreamland funfair: like being smacked around the head from all directions with an enormous neon-flashing cartoon hammer. And then being kicked repeatedly in the guts with comedy-clown shoes too. A giant Woody Woodpecker on some kind of mechanical spring, flailing and honking and stuttering maniacally towards us, a siren wailing from somewhere like it was the blitz. 'Relax' by Frankie Goes To Hollywood blaring from the dodgems, Madonna's 'Like A Virgin' pumping from the Hearts and Diamonds. Some bloke on a loudspeaker begging, 'Scream ladies, scream!' And everything drenched in that queasy white light.

Dad and Janice ambled off in the direction of the arcades. Esha and Bela made a bee-line for the dodgems, and Push was left to pair off with me. He marched me through the park, half dragging me by the arm to all the rides. I felt my responses become slower, everything I looked at drifted and shuddered for no reason at all and I felt like my arms and legs had bricks tied to them.

People with their kids laughing and arguing and stuffing candyfloss into their faces. Queues for the roller-coaster and a giant boat thing that rotated in the air. The stench of burgers and everything around me a blurred streak of noise and colour, fast then slow but random stuff illuminated, odd things suddenly clear and sharp. I spotted Dad and Janice by the Tea-cups ride, holding hands, saw a look of such tenderness pass between them I nearly fell over. I hadn't noticed, had been looking the other way to realise before, that they loved each other. A child crying because it had dropped its ice cream, its face one red and sweaty ball of anguish. A lad I'd seen working the dodgems was kissing Esha behind the hot-dog stall, his hand on her left tit. Bela smoked a fag next to them, looking bored.

Then Push was pulling me again by the wrist across hot, black, melting tarmac, my flip-flops sinking with each step. Queuing for what seemed like hours for the roller-coaster and then there we were. Hurtling up into that big blue sky, towards the blinding sun that every day Kyle said weighed a little less.

★　★　★

And suddenly I knew what had happened to Katie.

★　★　★

As we dipped and rose and swooped and spiralled high above the crowds of daytrippers, I knew. I knew with total certainty what had happened at No. 33 that night last summer.

★ ★ ★

The ride gradually slowed and ground to a halt and when the bar rose from my lap I followed Push along the shifting metal platform which seemed to have turned to water beneath my feet, and suddenly I was stepping off into nothing. Blackness rising over my eyeballs. My cheek against tarmac, my body sinking into nothingness and God knows how long I was on the ground for but gradually a pin-prick of light appeared and got steadily larger until black-rimmed sunshine filled my eyes again. My body was still stuck to the tarmac and I couldn't seem to find the strength to get up.

I became aware that I was surrounded by people's legs and, trying not to vomit, I looked up to see a ring of faces peering down on me with interest, like I was one of the more entertaining sideshows on the way to the big, rotating, boat thing. I could hear Push whining from miles away, 'She just fell! One minute she was standing up, next thing she was on the floor. Think she fainted. Weren't my fault.'

I rested my head on the tarmac again and stared instead at all the legs. Nobody really said or did anything and I grew strangely anxious that people might be finding me quite disappointing. I started to think about getting up, but couldn't actually picture how I'd manage it.

Finally the legs shuffled apart to make room for a pair of trousers I recognised. They were my dad's, the ones with the shiny knees and the falling-down hems, the ones he used to wear for the only job he'd ever had, when he worked the buses in Leeds. I looked up and there he was: my dad, pushing through the people, elbowing them all out the way, leaving Janice and Push trailing behind him. My dad. And as everyone stood and stared he knelt down and he picked me up and he carried me through the fair, out through the big gates, down along the beach, back through the town, all the way to the train station he carried me, my dad. The whole way there he held me in his arms in the heat and through the crowds and I rested my head against his chest and listened to the beating of my father's heart beneath his nylon cardigan.

A new single carriage, new writing on the walls. Me lying on one side, my family on the bench opposite. Watching me, their eyes agog, their mouths gaping, like I was something thrilling on the telly. So I closed my eyes and pretended to sleep and I listened to Janice and Dad whispering about the flu or how maybe it was 'women's things' and I thought about Kyle and what I knew, and suddenly I saw what needed to be done.

15

New Cross Hospital. 4 September 1986. Transcription of interview between Dr C Barton and Anita Naidu. Police copy.

I ran all the way. Through the back streets, past the gasworks and the power station, along the river. I ran all the way, through all the tourists, past the Cutty Sark and the markets. I didn't stop until I got to the police station and then everything stopped. It was the strangest thing. There I was, suddenly standing in that police station and everything went very quiet and I looked down and there was blood all over me, covering every bit of me, and I was still holding the bloody knife, Kyle's birthday knife. And all those coppers, just standing there so still and quiet, just staring at me, all those big men so frightened at the sight of me. And then I heard someone screaming, someone was screaming really loudly, and I realised it was me. And then all of a sudden was the shouting and the voices and the questions and then the sirens and the doctors, and then the quiet of the hospital room where they left me before they came at me again with their endless, endless questions. But the silence of that hospital bed was more horrible somehow than anything else and all I could think was, where was the shoe? Where was Katie's little shoe? Must have dropped it as I ran along the river. Must have dropped it as I ran.

So anyway, Denis went missing a couple of days later.

I had been to the shop to buy some sweets and was sitting on our front step as usual, sucking the fizz off my cola bottles and candy worms one by one. The sky seemed lower, thicker. It was still hot but now you could smell a distant coolness; a hint, just a warning of rain. It felt like when you watch a glass fall; that moment just before it hits the floor and shatters. I sat and waited.

I was thinking about something that had happened when I was little. One day my family went to the circus near where we lived in Hunslet. My best friend Susan Price came too and we sat in a vast chilly tent all in a row on a bench with peeling paint, I can still feel the warmth of my mother's arm around me, Susan's hand in mine. Next to me Push sat under a green bobble hat almost as big as him and my sisters wore matching duffle coats with white fluffy scarves.

My dad's breath was like smoke in the cold night air. We were all transfixed by the lights and the colours, the crack of the ringmaster's whip, the monkey so hilarious on his little red bike, the sequinned ladies dangling from a trapeze, the lions with their flashing eyes and teeth. We roared with laughter at the clowns and screamed when the tightrope man pretended to fall. And all around us, the bright lights and the enormous tent and the smell of toffee apples, roast chestnuts and sawdust and somewhere behind it all a brass band played.

Afterwards, in the rush to leave the tent, Susan and I got separated from the rest and were carried away in a sea of legs and coat hems. Suddenly Susan stumbled and fell, her hand landing on a broken beer bottle. My head was still full of lions and sawdust and clowns and crowds, of bright lights and trumpets, and when Susan held her hand up to show me the bloody shard of green glass jutting from her palm, her eyes huge and wet with shock, I could only stare, mesmerised, at the red blood and the green glass caught there in the half-light from a hotdog stand. The red blood, the white flesh, the green glass, gleaming and sparkling and beautiful in the dim light of a naked bulb.

I didn't think about it clearly, I just reached

out, my eyes still on the pretty colours, the red, the white, the green. And instead of pulling the shard out, I poked it in even further, hadn't meant to, but I couldn't help watching, fascinated, as the wound widened and spewed. I was oblivious to Susan's screams.

Suddenly my mother was behind me, picking up Susan, pulling the glass from her hand and wrapping it in a hanky, kissing and hugging her while Susan cried and cried. But I had only wanted to look at all the pretty shining colours, the red, the white, the green.

Sitting there on the step, I noticed eventually a figure in the distance. It was coming towards me from the direction of the main road. As I watched I realised that the person was walking strangely. First they'd scurry forwards at a rush, then they'd stop and continue more slowly. I watched them make their way up Myre Street in fits and starts like that for a while before I realised it was Denis's mum, Gloria. Despite the heat she was buttoned up in a thick black coat, a blue bonnet perched stiffly on top of her Playmobil hair.

When she got level with Kyle's house she stopped at the front gate. I noticed that she was talking to herself, that she kept making the same gesture with her hand, reaching up as if to pat her hat down more firmly on her head. She kept lurching forward as if to go in through Kyle's front gate, but each time she attempted it something would stop her in her tracks.

Eventually she looked wildly around her. That's when she spotted me. As she scuttled over I realised suddenly that she was crying.

'Anita,' she said, and I shrank back because she reminded me a bit of that dog Tiffany from the scrapyard, and I was afraid that she might bite me.

'Have you seen Denis?' Her West Indian accent was much stronger when she was upset.

'No,' I said. 'Not since the other day when we went swimming with Kyle.'

At the mention of his name she made a sucking sound with her teeth. 'That Kyle knows where he is.' She nodded bitterly over to No. 33. Then she blurted desperately in a rush of tears, 'Haven't seen Denny since yesterday. Thought he was in bed when I got back. Thought he was asleep and I didn't check. Not there this morning when I took him up his milk.' She stopped and slowly shook her head in disbelief at the memory of her shock. 'He's never not there. And he hasn't turned up neither and it's nearly twelve o'clock. He ain't got no other friends apart from you and him' (she nodded over to Kyle's door) 'and I'm going to find out right now where he's got to.'

She glared at me as if I was going to try and stop her and when I just shrugged, she rolled her eyes and off she went. She launched herself across the road and almost threw herself at Kyle's door and though she could barely reach the knocker she started banging it as if to wake the dead. Eventually the big black door opened, and after watching her shout at him for a bit, Patrick, looking baffled, stood aside to let her in.

I waited and after ten minutes the door opened again and she came hurtling out, crying still. Kyle and Patrick gazed after her from their step as she flung herself back down Myre Street — straight to Brockley police station as it turned out, though I didn't know that then. I only knew I didn't have much time to lose. Kyle and Patrick looked at each other, shrugged, and made to go back inside. I was on Kyle's front step in seconds.

'Kyle.'

He closed the door gently behind Patrick, and walked to the pavement with me.

'All right?' he said.

The flapping bird feeling in my chest. 'I need to show you something.' My voice sounded breathless and strange.

'What's the matter with you?' he asked.

'I need to show you something,' I said again.

He considered me for a few moments, then looked off down the street at Gloria's retreating back. 'You seen Denis?' he asked. 'His mum just went mental at us.' A flicker of enjoyment on his face.

I was trying to keep calm but almost shouted, 'Kyle, you've got to come with me now!'

He looked at me like I was mad. I lowered my voice, told myself to get a grip. 'Please, Kyle. You've got to come down to the river. It's important.'

He stared at me for a while longer then shrugged. He seemed tired, distracted. 'OK.'

We started walking to the bus stop. Occasionally he'd throw me puzzled glances and say, 'What's going on, Anita? Where are we going?' But when I didn't answer, he gave up, and we got on the bus in silence.

Through the backstreets I took him, down to the Thames. The few people that we passed were frowning expectantly up at the thickening sky and again there was that sense of distant rain, that strange feeling of watching a falling glass just before it hits the ground and shatters. The world held its breath.

We followed the river for a while, the

214

receding tide revealing its vomited bounty of mud and driftwood, plastic bags, empty bottles, a broken tricycle. Through the empty wastelands I took him, filled with those musky white flowers, the ones that smell of cats' piss, of summer. Past the factories, the warehouses, past our hideout, past the point where the river twists, through a gap between some hardboard and corrugated iron, into the empty scrapyard.

The sky was still blue but a little less so, like the colour had been stretched out of it; a blue balloon that has been blown too big.

'Why've you brought me here, Anita?' He looked around the empty yard in surprise. He gazed at me expectantly, a little irritated. 'Well? Why have you brought me all this way?'

He crouched on the floor. He hadn't noticed the mound of earth at the far end.

I knew that I was right, I knew that Kyle and I were the same and that he would love me for what I was about to show him, but still my heart thumped nervously in my chest. Still I gulped and stuttered over my words as I began.

'I saw you, Kyle.'

He blinked at me, not understanding. Shook his head and shrugged. 'Saw me where?'

I sat down next to him. 'I saw you, the other day, in that little room off your kitchen.

I saw you,' I stopped, unable to look at him while I said it. 'I saw what you were doing with Patrick.'

When he didn't answer for a while, I looked up to watch the meaning of my words creep slowly across his face the way the putrid river creeps across the shore.

I stared again at the ground in front of me until the silence became so unbearable I dragged my eyes back to Kyle's face. It was ashen, demolished, every trace of blood drained from his skin. And when he turned his eyes to me they were full of shame.

He looked away and stared into the distance, nodding slowly to himself. The world flexed and waited. I knew I had to make him understand. I had to try and explain it all to him. But everything seemed broken and foul suddenly between us and I didn't know how to make him see.

And then I thought about what I'd done for him and I felt my heart might explode with excitement.

'It's all right,' I said. Gently I reached out and patted him on the arm. He flinched so violently he fell backwards. We stared at each other. Finally he sighed and got up. 'So?'

I looked at him and got up too.

'So?' he said again and his voice was cold and hard. 'What the fuck have you brought me here for? What the fuck do you *want*, Anita? Now you know. Did you just bring me here to tell me that?' He wouldn't look at me.

'No,' I whispered. I felt tears sting my eyes. I'd planned what I was going to say so carefully over the last couple of days, and now it was all going wrong. 'I know about Katie,' I said, just blurting it out.

He looked around him in exasperation. '*Katie?*' he said. 'What are you talking about?' He came up to me and stuck his face in mine and I flinched. 'What the fuck do you think you know about Katie?'

'It's OK,' I said, and I knew it was, I knew that he'd understand as soon as I showed him. I smiled and he recoiled from me. 'That's why I brought you here,' I said, and I gestured to the mound of earth. 'I found it, Kyle. I found the old sand mine for you.'

He looked from me to the mound with amazement. 'You what?' he asked.

I savoured the moment. 'I found it, Kyle. I found the mine for you,' I said.

He went over to it then, his eyes still on me as he began to pull the boards and girders from its mouth. When he saw the hole his face lit up with excitement. 'I don't believe it!' he said, his expression almost making me cry with happiness.

217

I felt brave enough then to say, 'Kyle, I know that you killed Katie.'

'What?' He was only half paying attention, so desperate was he to explore the mine.

'I know you killed Katie,' I said again.

He dropped the bit of hardboard he was holding, came back to where I was standing. I felt nervous again at the expression on his face, but told myself it was OK: I'd known it was going to be hard for him to talk about it at first. But I knew that once he realised how much I loved him and that we were the same then everything would be OK.

I took a deep breath. 'I know you killed her to protect her from Patrick.'

He stared at me for what seemed like ages. I braced myself for his reaction. I had expected tears and then a confession. And love, I had expected love. But he just carried on looking at me with something like horror. Seconds dripped by.

'Killed her?' he said, his voice very faint.

I nodded and took hold of his arm. 'But it's OK, Kyle. It's OK. I love you.'

He shook me off like ants. Finally he said, slowly and carefully as if to a retarded person, 'Anita. I didn't kill my sister. What the fuck is the matter with you? Nobody *kills* people. Are you completely mad? This isn't TV. My sister's in America with Dad.'

I sat down on the ground, my legs feeling very weak suddenly. I tried to piece things together. My head felt very thick and confused. Nothing made sense. Eventually Kyle came and sat down beside me.

He took a deep breath and put his head in his hands. It was a while before he spoke. 'She saw us,' he said. 'Katie. She saw me and Granddad.' I looked at him, but he wouldn't meet my eyes. 'He's been doing it since I was a kid.' Neither of us spoke for a while and I heard Kyle begin to cry. Raspy, reedy sobs. Finally he wiped his tears away with his bony little hand. 'He said that if my mum ever found out that it would kill her. And it would have done. I know it would.'

I had no idea what to say, he still wasn't making any sense.

'She couldn't take it,' Kyle whispered. 'Granddad told me.' He started crying again. 'When he, when it first started, I was about five. He said that it would kill her to know about us, and it would all be my fault because I'd made him do it.'

I thought about the look on Elizabeth's face, that frightened, guilty expression, the day I'd seen her on the stairs.

'One day Katie came in and saw us, and I was so fucking scared that she'd tell Mum. I told Katie not to but she didn't really understand. She loved me though, you know? She'd do anything I said.' A brief smile. 'But I knew it was only a matter of time before she slipped up. She wouldn't have meant to, but sooner or later she would have said something to Mum.' Kyle exhaled and wiped some snot off his nose with his jumper.

'My dad wanted us to live with him but he wasn't allowed to have us. He'd been to court and everything, tried everything to get us back. So I phoned him, I snuck out and phoned him and we arranged it. I helped him kidnap Katie, Anita.' He turned to me, horrified. 'It was me.'

'Why didn't you go too?' I whispered.

'I had to look after Mum,' he said. 'Granddad's not there all the time. I couldn't leave her on her own. She couldn't cope.'

He stopped talking then, just stared down at his hands. He was lost in thought for a few moments, remembering. 'She cried so much, when I took her to meet Dad that night. She didn't want to go. She knew she'd never see Mum or me again. I told her that she would but she knew it wasn't true. She was crying, begging me to take her back home. She didn't understand, she thought she'd done something wrong and that me and Mum didn't want her any more. But I knew I had to. I knew it was for the best. I had to do it.'

I tried to make sense of what he was telling me.

'But,' I said. 'But, I thought . . . Mike, and everything, I thought.'

He looked at me then. 'What, Anita? You thought what? That just because I'd given that cunt Mike what for, that I'd be up for murdering my kid sister?' He shook his head. 'You're fucking barking, you really are.'

As I looked at Kyle I felt the world and all its people, every single one, disappear. Even Kyle didn't seem real to me any more. I felt every single human being vanish until it was just me, just me alone in the whole universe. Like one of those sea birds, that's how I felt then. Tearing through empty skies above empty oceans, nothing, no one in sight.

Kyle wiped the tears and snot from his face, got up and went over to the hole. I followed him, watched him pick up the torch I'd left just outside, saw him turn it on and smile, watched him bend down and crawl through. I stood at the mouth while he lowered himself down the steps. I watched him straighten up and shine the light around the cave, waited for his beam to find Mike and Denis.

Heard him say in a voice like shattered glass, 'Oh shit.'

16

I'd put my plan into action a few days before. It really wasn't my fault that Denis had got himself involved. I hadn't meant for it to turn out that way at all.

It had actually been less complicated to find Mike than I thought it would be. I'd imagined myself hanging around in the alley outside his estate for hours, just waiting for him to pass by. I braced myself for the possibility of him turning up with all his mates because I knew that would have been me fucked; they'd have kicked my head in for sure. I knew it, but I went anyway. I had no choice. As it turned out though I bumped into Mike straightaway. He was alone and heading towards me. Lucky, or what?

He didn't even notice me standing there. In fact he would have walked straight past me if I hadn't called out to him. He looked up when he heard his name and as soon as he recognised me he tensed and stopped and I realised that he was looking around for Kyle. Now that he was close to me I could see that he had bruises on his face and neck, and I wondered who'd given them to him. He was wearing a bright pink T-shirt that made his see-through skin and greasy hair look even sicker than usual.

'Mike,' I said again, to his stupid face that gaped at me like I'd just landed from Mars.

'Hah?' he said, and we stood there for a few moments while I let the penny drop.

'Where's your mate?' he said at last.

'Kyle?' I said. 'That's why I'm here. He wants to meet you. He wants me to take you to him.'

'Fuck off.'

'Seriously,' I said, trotting after him, because he'd begun to walk away. 'He says he wants to finish what he started.'

Mike stopped walking. He laughed his shrill girl's laugh. 'Are you fucking serious?'

I shrugged.

'Why don't the big man come down here and do it then?'

I became very aware suddenly of all the different textures of Mike. His white-blond hair, his scabby mouth, his lurid T-shirt. I remember thinking that though he was only fifteen and skinny, he still looked strong, with an evil sort of strength that came from somewhere rotten in him. But it was the innocent quality to his face that made him really terrifying. That stupid, childlike expression that chilled you to the fucking bone

223

when you spotted the cruelty hiding there below the surface, like a razor blade in chocolate.

I tried to keep my nerve. 'He reckons you'll have all your mates with you if he comes down here,' I said, as casually as I could.

He considered this for a bit, shook his head, spat somewhere near my foot, then walked on. 'Haven't got time for this,' he said. 'Gotta get down the offy for me mum.'

I waited until he'd walked a few steps. Then I said quietly, 'Yeh, he told me you'd be too chicken-shit to meet him.'

He moved so quickly I hardly knew what was happening. He spun back on himself and in one movement he had hold of my neck and was marching me back down the alley. His fingers were digging so hard into my throat I started coughing. He bent down and whispered in my ear, 'Right you are then, Paki. Take me to your boyfriend and I'll punch his fucking teeth in.' He kicked me in the back of the knees. 'Then I'll punch yours in too.' It was like every muscle in his body was concentrated in his fingertips and I thought that they were going to go right through my neck. I couldn't breathe.

He marched me through the alley, only releasing his grip when we came out onto the busy traffic of Blackheath Hill. 'Where now?' he asked.

I couldn't make my voice work properly for a few seconds, and he kicked me in the knee again, making my leg buckle. I rubbed my throat.

'We've gotta get on a bus to Greenwich,' I said. 'Near the river.' And I half hoped that he'd lose interest and go away. Then I looked at his face, and I knew that he wasn't going anywhere. He was enjoying himself too much.

He nodded, grabbed my shoulder and pushed me in the direction of the bus stop. He walked a few steps behind me the whole way, kicking me in the back of the legs occasionally to let me know he was still there. When we got on the bus he sat a couple of seats away and I kept my eyes fixed on him. Just before we had to get off, I saw him do something that almost made my heart stop. He glanced around to check that no one was looking, then pulled a flick-knife from his pocket. He held it between his knees, half crouching over it, and pressed the catch to make it spring open. Then he closed it, lovingly stroked the black plastic handle and put it back in his pocket.

'We're here,' I said, thinking fuck-fuck-fuck-fuck, thinking what the fuck do I do now? He nodded and we got off and walked together down the backstreets where we'd seen him and his mates that time at the beginning of the summer, and all the way I wondered what I should do, now that I knew he had a knife. I hadn't banked on that at all. I hadn't taken that into account. But there was really nothing for it but to stick to my original plan. So, with Mike complaining the entire way, I led him to the mine.

We stood in the middle of the empty scrapyard, and he said, 'Come on then, Bud-bud-ding-ding, where's the big man?' I jerked my head in the direction of the mound of earth on the other side, and told him to follow me. He sighed and said, 'Seriously, you're going to fucking get it if he doesn't turn up.' I nodded, my throat dry, and started to pull the girders and boards from the hole. As he watched me, he pulled out his knife again and flicked it open. Suddenly my mind focused. I pulled the flashlight out of its hiding place where I'd left it the day before, and without turning it on I dived through the hole into the cave. Scrabbling down the steps in the dark, I heard Mike say from near the mouth, 'What the fuck? Is this a cave?' And then a moment later, 'Cool!' He sounded like an excited kid.

I knew he'd follow me. He had the knife, he felt safe. I knew he'd come. I put the torch

226

on the floor. Waited for him. My eyes had grown accustomed to the dark by then. His hadn't. He felt his way into the little chamber, it glowed yellow in the torchlight. 'Wow. This is fucking all right.' He squinted at me. 'OK, Bud-bud, nice of you to show me where you and your family live and all that, but now let's go and find your mate,' he grinned, the knife in his hand, 'so I can cut his ears off.'

He turned to go, then stopped when I said, 'In here'. He gave me a suspicious look and I nodded to the little passageway that led to the next chamber of the mine. 'What?' he said. He walked towards me. The faces carved into the sandy walls gazed down on him, unnoticed.

I nodded at the opening. 'He's in there,' I said.

He pushed me aside, then slipped into the narrow passage. 'I can't see a fucking thing,' he complained.

There's nothing that momentous about killing someone, not really. You think there'd be more to it. I had Kyle's penknife open in a second. Pushed the biggest blade into Mike's side while he was caught in the narrow opening, before he even knew what was happening. Like cutting into a tomato. Surprising, though, the blood, how warm it is. How much of it there is. Funny that he didn't even know he was dying at first. Susan, my friend, she'd known at once. She knew she was going to die. Maybe that's why I enjoyed it more. Or maybe that was just because I'd loved her so much.

Mike turned and his face, in the off-kilter beam from the torch on the floor made his eyes look like hollows, long shadows under each one. He turned and gave me the strangest look, batted vaguely with his hand where I'd put the knife in. I stabbed him again. He felt that, fell forward, dropping his own knife. 'Wha — ?' he said. 'Wha — ?'

I stabbed him again, I stabbed him right in his heart. The newspapers said later that he'd been knifed seventeen times, but I'm sure they were exaggerating. Punctured like a wet beach ball, blood came from his mouth, from everywhere, it took him a while to die. I sat cross-legged on the floor and watched. What did I feel? I felt nothing. Only that a tightness in me became suddenly a little less.

I had done what I'd gone there to do. I had killed Mike, for Kyle, I had killed Mike but it didn't feel as good as I thought it was going to: to be honest I felt a little empty. Not how I'd felt before.

It began when I was six. Susan Price was my best friend and we went everywhere together. We sat next to each other in school and stayed over at each other's houses at the weekend. I loved her long red hair and her freckles and I used to wish I had sky-blue eyes like she did. I'd even get my mum to buy me the same clothes as hers. And when I stayed at her house we'd sleep side by side in our matching pyjamas, side by side in the same bed. We'd have midnight feasts and I used to say, 'What are you thinking? What are you thinking right now?' Because it frightened me that I didn't know exactly what she thought and felt every minute of every day. What it felt like to be her.

The world had started to feel very big to me when I was six. Whenever I thought about its vastness, about how many people there were living in it, I'd start to get a tight, panicky feeling in my chest. I'd often dream that I was drowning in people, that I was in the middle of a huge crowd of strangers and they were clambering over me, squashing and trampling and smothering me until eventually there was nothing left of me, and when I'd wake up, breathless and afraid, the fear that I had never entirely went.

And sometimes I couldn't sleep for thinking about the amount of people in the world, about all the different thoughts and feelings in their heads and how I'd never know them, nor them me. I'd see a person on the street; just a random person — an old man, a kid, anyone — and I'd stare and stare at them, driving myself mad with thinking about them because the more I wondered about them, the less real I became, the less I could see myself, feel myself, and then the terror would start. Suddenly I seemed to be always outside myself, could only see Anita from the outside, as if I was another person watching myself, wondering who I was. And it scared me, it absolutely terrified me. Eventually, even my own voice frightened me because when I'd speak to someone, I would watch them react to me and answer me and that didn't make any sense because I couldn't work out who it was they were replying to, who they were looking at, whose voice they heard.

When I used to stay round Susan's house and she'd fall asleep, I'd watch her chest rise and fall, rise and fall. I'd want to know so badly what she was dreaming about, what it felt like to be her. Sometimes I'd wake her up and ask her, 'What were you dreaming about? What were you dreaming about just then?' And she'd push me away and say, 'Nothing, go back to sleep.' But I'd lie there and I'd stare at her and I'd try to stop the panic rising.

I loved Susan. I loved her so much. I loved her gappy teeth and the sound of her laugh and the redness of her eyebrows. I wanted to spend every second with her, I wanted to know what it felt like to be her, what it was like inside her skin. I thought I'd be real again if I could just know what that felt like even for a second. And it got so that need in me got bigger than me, it became me, do you know what I mean?

One morning at school our teacher gave us our little bottles of milk with the blue straws and Susan and I went to the Wendy house in the corner of the playground to drink them. Inside was this cot thing, like a camp bed, and Susan lay on it while I sat on the floor. She was giggling about something, I don't remember what. The yelling squealing shouting of the other kids in the playground was like a crazy bubbling sea that kept threatening to crash into our little house, our hot, orange little world that smelt of sweaty grass and baked plastic; crash in and sweep away the last remaining specs of me. I tried to concentrate, to focus, to cling on to the real solid fact of Susan like a drowning person clings to a raft.

After a while Susan's eyes began to flutter closed and she began to fall asleep. I watched her little body fall and rise, fall and rise and

231

suddenly I couldn't bear it, that buzzing like a million wasps behind my eyes, that screeching like a million people trapped inside my head. Suddenly, Doctor Barton, I had the sensation of being in a very dark tunnel, and at the end of the tunnel was a brilliant light that I needed desperately to get to. Everything went black, suddenly, black and silent, only Susan, asleep on the bed was visible. She glowed, Doctor Barton, she glowed.

I didn't think about it clearly. An instinct made me do it, told me how to do it. I got up and I went over to the little cot. I put my fingers on her neck. She woke up with a start and for a moment we stared into each other's eyes. I covered her mouth with my hand, and still her eyes held mine. I put my fingers into her throat and pressed, and then I lent on her neck with all my might, using my other hand to cover her mouth and nose. And all the time she didn't make a sound — she thrashed and struggled under me but she didn't make a sound and her eyes never left mine.

And it felt beautiful. As I looked into her eyes I knew for the first time exactly what she was feeling. As she stopped struggling and I felt the Susan-ness leave her and fill me up, I felt complete. A whole person, not just a nothing, empty person, not the shadowy, confused, frightened person I'd always been.

No, I felt connected and certain and real in the world for the first time ever. And just for a moment, the whole world became perfectly light, so light it hurt my eyes.

My teacher found us. Susan had her eyes closed, and she'd gone a funny colour, but she was still breathing. I'll never forget the expression on my teacher's face.

I was asked to leave that school. My mum came and collected me twenty minutes later and I never went back. And I never saw Susan again, though my mum said she'd told everyone we were only playing.

So I stayed at home for a while, under my mother's careful watch. And though she'd say, 'You *were* just playing, weren't you? You'd never hurt your little friend!' I saw a haunted, sickened look creep into her eyes from that day onward that never really left her.

And every night I would go to sleep thinking about how wonderful I had felt, that day in the Wendy house with Susan. All I could think about was how much I wanted to feel that again, how desperately I needed to feel that again.

★   ★   ★

There in the sand mine I pulled the knife out of Mike and wiped it on my jeans. I felt empty. I had killed him for Kyle, to show him that I was the same as him, would do anything for him. And I had expected to feel how I had felt with Susan, I thought it would be the same, that the beauty would return. But killing Mike had felt like nothing. And a cold seeping blackness started to fill every single part of me until eventually I really couldn't see the difference anymore between me and the cold, dead, black air of the mine.

I shone my torch on Mike's body, lying punctured and wrecked there on the sandy floor. It didn't matter, I told myself. It really didn't matter; I had done it all for Kyle, I had done it for Kyle and now I could tell him about it and he could tell me about how he'd killed Katie and we could run away together. To the sea, to America, to anywhere. Everything would make sense as soon as I told Kyle.

When I came out of the mine, blinking at the sudden sunshine, I hadn't even had time to change into the spare clothes I'd brought when I saw Denis appear through the gap in the fence at the far end of the scrapyard. I froze in shock while he bounded over to me, his fat lips flopping open like a big fish. Glub, glub, glub. 'Hah?' he said. 'You just came out of the ground!' He looked at me with amazement like I was some sort of magician.

He ducked his head so he could peer around me. 'What's that hole?' he asked.

'Denis,' I said. 'What are you doing here?' I wondered how I was going to explain my blood-stained clothes.

'I saws you!' he said. 'From the bus! I saws you and Kyle!'

I stared at him. 'Denis, where are your glasses?' His eyes without his specs looked like tiny white marbles sunken into his big chubby face.

'I left them at home' he said. 'I broke them.' He grinned. 'I saws you and Kyle from the bus. So I got off but you were really far away but I followed you. I followed you the whole way. I was like James Bond.' His face clouded over. 'Then I lost you.' He brightened again. 'Then I thought to myself, you must be in here, cos there's nowhere else you could have gone. So I looked through a gap and then I came in! But you weren't here and — '

'Denis,' I interrupted him, knowing that this could go on all day. 'I wasn't with Kyle. That was Mike.'

He shook his head stubbornly. 'Course you were with Kyle,' he said. 'I saws you. I *saws* you!'

Denis always said saws instead of saw. Fucking irritating it was.

'No you didn't,' I said patiently. 'That was Mike. I was with Mike. Come on, Denis,' I said. 'Let's go home.'

But he was having none of it. 'Nah though. You ain't friends with Mike.' He ran up to the hole. 'Is it a cave? Have you and Kyle found a cave?'

'No, Denis. Come on, let's go home,' I said.

He looked at me like I was playing tricks on him and then he laughed. 'Kyle's in there, isn't he?' he said.

I couldn't persuade him, I couldn't make him listen. I did try, honestly I did. He just wouldn't take any notice. Not surprising I suppose, seeing as that was what the three of us had been looking for all summer. 'I wanna go in,' he whined. 'I wanna go in.'

'Don't,' I said. 'It's dark and it's small and you hate being underground, remember?' But he wouldn't have it. He pushed past me and peeked in.

'I'll just go in for a bit. See Kyle.' He pushed his head further into the cave's mouth. 'Kyle!' he said excitedly. 'Kyle, are you in there?' He grabbed the torch from the ground where I'd left it, and turned it on.

I picked up a rock and followed him.

Inside the mine Denis was shining the torch on Mike. He had his fingers in his mouth. 'Anita,' he was saying. 'Anita,' he said and his voice was very small. He knelt down to look at Mike more closely. Started to shake him by the shoulder. 'Anita,' he said. 'Anita, someone's killed Mike.'

I hit Denis with my rock. It left a big gaping cut on his forehead and knocked him out. And when I stabbed him in his big flabby gut, I felt nothing.

17

A few moments after Kyle went into the mine the sky bagged and belched then sweated slow and heavy drops of rain that landed on me and the ground like balls of sodden tissue. Splat, splat, splat.

I followed Kyle and found him standing next to Denis, the torch in his hand. I didn't like the way he was looking at me. Like he didn't know me.

'Anita,' he was saying. 'What have you done?' His face looked drawn and scared in the torchlight. He knelt down next to Denis. Traced the wound on his forehead. 'Denis,' he whispered. 'Fucking hell, Anita, what have you done?'

I looked at him. 'I did it for you.'

'Why?' he said. '*Why?*' He touched Denis's springy hair and whimpered, 'I don't understand, Anita. I don't understand why you've done this.' And he kept shaking his head. Suddenly he was crying. Big fat oozing tears. I watched them catch on his cheek then fall onto Denis. 'You're crazy, Anita. You're really, really crazy,' he whispered. 'I mean, what's going to happen now, what are you going to do now? This is fucking mad. You killed Denis and Mike, Anita. You fucking killed them.'

I searched his eyes for recognition, for understanding; some sort of connection and acceptance.

'I did it for you,' I said desperately. 'I killed Mike for you, to show you that I understood about Katie, and that we can run away together if you want. We can do whatever we want now because we're the same. I did it all for you.' I didn't know what else to say because Kyle was just staring at me, appalled. He didn't love me. We weren't the same. It was all fucking wrong.

'Anita,' he said. 'You've got to get help, man. We've got to go and get help.'

Like someone had flicked a switch and the world was entirely empty. Just me, just me in the darkness.

It didn't matter, it didn't matter, I pulled the knife from my pocket, opened it one last time. And suddenly Kyle was rushing at me with the rock I'd hit Denis with. But in that last second he faltered, and the rock didn't hit me as hard as it could have done. It scuffed my head and I stumbled backwards. Kyle dived past me and in that instant the cave that had been so cool and wonderful and full of promise, my lovely secret, my present

239

to Kyle, felt all at once a hot and crazy place thick with the smell of Mike and Denis's blood and Kyle's disgust. He was leaving me and we would never be together.

So as he passed me I stuck the knife into his neck. Stuck it in right up to its shiny red handle. He fell towards me, onto me, and I collapsed with him in my arms. And just like Susan he looked right into my eyes. As his neck bubbled red and the blood ran onto my hand, he looked right into me. His breathing was ragged, quick and gaspy. As I cradled his head I stared at his eyes and I felt such love, I felt such love. I wasn't alone any more.

Such a lot of blood. His throat pulsed and gurgled and soon both of us were soaked. I felt whole and strong. Through the thin, wet material of his T-shirt I felt his heart beneath my bloody palm falter trip then stop. And at the moment he left himself he entered me like I was water. Do you know what I mean? Do you understand? He was me, finally, he was mine, and that made me real.

All summer long I had studied every detail of him like I used to do with Susan. His nobbly bony head, the way his left foot turned in slightly when he walked, the freckles on his white white skin, the different textures of his voice. And now all those little bits that made up Kyle, that made him him, were leaving Kyle and becoming part of me. I held him in my arms and I stroked his head until finally, finally his eyes became still and he was mine.

18

I sat with Kyle for ages, his body cold and limp across my lap. And while all those empty eyes gazed down on us I carefully etched the words Denis, Kyle, Anita on the floor with Kyle's penknife, my grip slipping and sliding over the bloody handle. I have never been back, but I know they are still there, those words. I know we are all still down there.

I never found out what happened to Patrick and Elizabeth. Push says the house has been empty ever since. I didn't go to Denis's funeral, though Gloria asked me to. And all through the endless questions from the endless policemen, all through the newspaper stories and the television debates, the how-how-hows, the why-why-whys, the outcry and the revulsion, through the excitement and the boo-hoo-hoos (how they picked Kyle's bones dry, how they savoured every drop). Through it all: the memory, my sweet treasured memory of the glorious relief of knowing, even briefly, what it felt like to be a whole, real person, to be connected and involved and certain — for the first time ever not frightened and invisible; not a nothing, hungry person anymore.

The days pass like the Thames, steady and inevitable. On my way to the factory I watch the school kids on my bus. They look so similar in their little uniforms, don't they? Occasionally I'll see a quiet one, separate from the rest and I'll wonder about the secrets that he keeps. I think often, always, of Kyle, and I cherish the memory of the two of us that last day, that end-of-summer day, that end-of-everything day when I was thirteen. But over the past few years it's been getting harder to hold on to, harder to remember.

Nobody doubted me. The police didn't like Kyle. His teachers didn't like Kyle. Gloria didn't even question that it might not be him who had murdered her son. I had the cuts on my head from the rock. It was easy. There were even witnesses who, from the windows of the estate, had seen what had happened in the alley the time Kyle stabbed Mike. I told the police what I'd seen him doing with Patrick and that put the extra doubt in their mind. He was a fucked-up kid. Katie's disappearance had lingered over No. 33 like dried vomit for a year, so the little shoe in Kyle's chest at the hide-out, plus the one I said I'd found in the mine sealed the deal. It didn't matter when I said I'd dropped it in the Thames as I ran to the police. I was a good, quiet girl. I stuck to my story. I had killed Kyle in self-defence. They believed me. They wanted to.

Everybody except you, Doctor Barton.

What was it? Which bit of my story gave me away? Which part of my act failed to convince?

Do you remember that room in New Cross Hospital? That spider plant, yellow-leaved and queasy, those too-close, lime-coloured walls? With the windows open it was too loud, the buses interfering with your tape recorder. Trapped air, trapped heat, trapped light. It smelt of coffee and Dettol, didn't it? Eventually I talked and talked, said the words that over the years would embed themselves in your mind like metal wire wrapped tight around your brain.

The story of Kyle, the story of Kyle and me.

It was cruel of the police to use your expertise so carelessly, to move you off the case so quickly once your purpose had been served. You told me in that kind and quiet voice of yours that you'd been a child psychiatrist for years. You were there to assess, record, report. Your professional opinion had been sought. But it shocked you still, didn't it, my tale? Sickened you.

You didn't believe me.

But if you shared your doubts with the police, they clearly disregarded them. The evidence was stacked, it was such a straightforward if unpleasant case and you were only one of many professionals involved. But anyway, it makes no difference now. Since that day I have been very careful. You have had no cause to worry, to write to me so anxiously over the years. I have kept myself in check. The dial turned up to Freeze.

Until now. Until Malcolm.

He came round the day before yesterday. We sat here and watched a documentary about camels. When he left, he did the thing I'd longed for and been dreading for the past six weeks. At the door he stopped and he leant over and he kissed me. He kissed me right on the lips. And then he legged it down the corridor to his flat and he let himself in as fast as he could.

I can think of nothing but my desire to touch him, Doctor Barton, to stroke his sandy hair, to kiss his serious, slightly down-turned mouth. For him to touch me, too. And the more I want him, the more I think how wonderful it would be when he's sitting here next to me on my little sofa watching telly, to press my fingers to his neck, to slide a knife between his ribs. How beautiful that would be; how much love I could show him then.

When he kissed me that night, I went and sat in the bottom of my airing cupboard with my arms wrapped tight around my head and I crouched there in the dark for the rest of the night. And I wanted Malcolm to come back, I so wanted him, the one person I could never be alone with again.

Because, for an instant there, in that mine all those years ago, for just one brief second in that dark cold cave when I held Kyle in my arms and felt his blood soak every bit of me; suddenly there in the blackness there was so much light, such a pure, dazzling glare, for a moment there was almost too much light to see.

Help me, Doctor Barton. Can you help me please?

Acknowledgements

Thanks to: my agent Claire Paterson at Janklow & Nesbit and to Susan Watt and her team at HarperCollins.

Thanks also to: the Greenwich History Library, Rachel Pask, Tessa Paul, Ian Elliot, Ben Way, Mat Smith, Craig Glenday, Paul Croughton, Danny Patijn, Will Storr, William Drew and all my lovely colleagues at Arena magazine.

Special thanks to: Alex Cree, Dave Holloway, Justin Quirk and Anna Way.

We do hope that you have enjoyed reading this large print book.

Did you know that all of our titles are available for purchase?

We publish a wide range of high quality large print books including:
Romances, Mysteries, Classics
General Fiction
Non Fiction and Westerns

Special interest titles available in large print are:
The Little Oxford Dictionary
Music Book
Song Book
Hymn Book
Service Book

Also available from us courtesy of Oxford University Press:
Young Readers' Dictionary
(large print edition)
Young Readers' Thesaurus
(large print edition)

For further information or a free brochure, please contact us at:
Ulverscroft Large Print Books Ltd.,
The Green, Bradgate Road, Anstey,
Leicester, LE7 7FU, England.
Tel: (00 44) 0116 236 4325
Fax: (00 44) 0116 234 0205

Other titles published by
The House of Ulverscroft:

UNSTOLEN

Wendy Jean

The thing about being the unstolen one is that you'd better not rock any boats: people who can't take any more stress in their lives depend on you. And because, after all, you weren't taken, you'd better be grateful for everything you've had — your brother sure didn't get anything . . . Bethany Fisher has always lived in the shadow of her missing brother. Four-year-old Michael was abducted when Bethany was a baby, and no trace of him was ever found. Now a college graduate with a small son of her own, Bethany's life is thrown into turmoil when her mild-mannered mother suddenly snaps . . .

WEEKEND

William McIlvanney

A group of lecturers and students arrives on the Scottish island of Cannamore for a study weekend. Away from his wife, David Cudlipp feels free to seduce one of his students; Harry Beck seeks distraction from his stalled writing career; whilst Andrew Lawson rests from caring for his bed-ridden wife. Among the students, Kate Foster plans to lose her virginity and Jacqui Forsyth to recover from a break-up; while for Vikki Kane, it's a chance to shed her inhibitions. Then there's Marion, the 'Mouse', who plans only to observe everyone else. But nothing turns out quite how anyone expected . . .

THE TWISTING VINE

Margaret Muir

In Yorkshire, Lucy Oldfield works as a maid at Heaton Hall. But when Lord Farnley's daughter dies, a shadow is cast over its future . . . Feeling insecure and unable to overcome temptation, Lucy steals an expensive French doll from her dead mistress. When the Hall is put up for sale and the staff dismissed, Lucy returns to Leeds. There, she falls victim to the deceit of an admirer, finding herself with a child to support. And then a chance meeting with a gentleman on a train leads to an offer that appears to be too good to be true . . . But will Lucy find herself subjected to even more heartache?

BETWEEN, GEORGIA

Joshilyn Jackson

Nonny Frett understands the meanings of 'rock' and 'hard place'. While her husband is easing out the back door her best friend is laying siege to her heart in her front yard. Working in the city, she's addicted to a little girl deep in the country. Nonny has two families: the Fretts, who stole her and raised her right, and the Crabtrees, who lost her and can't forget they've been done wrong. Now in Between, Georgia, population 90, a thirty-year-old stash of highly flammable secrets is about to be ignited — and Nonny is sitting in the middle of it . . .

AFTER MICHAEL

Betty O'Rourke

Fiona Latimer learns that her husband Michael has died of a heart attack alone in his London flat. She is shocked but not devastated; they had led separate lives for some years. Two people arrive at the funeral, each with considerable influence on future events. Anthea is a girl who knows more about Michael than she will admit, and Simon is someone from Fiona's past, whom she now realises she should have married instead. Gradually, secrets from Michael's past are uncovered and the final, shocking betrayals are revealed. Fiona now discovers her life with him was not at all what it had seemed . . .

THE HALF LIFE OF STARS

Louise Wener

Claire's older brother has disappeared. He leaves work one afternoon, and vanishes into thin air. Married, successful, with seemingly no reason to abandon his life, has he been killed? Or has he just had enough? This story of a family with ghosts to bury opens on the day of the Challenger shuttle explosion at Cape Canaveral, a tragic moment that rips this family apart and sets in motion Daniel's disappearance eighteen years later. In the midst of it all sits Claire — promiscuous, irresponsible, hopeless at interpreting life — who knows Daniel best. And it's Claire who sets off to find him . . .